The play's the thing.

I have heard that guilty creatures sitting at a play
Have by the very cunning of the scene
Been struck so to the soul that presently
They have proclaimed their malefactions.
For murder, though it have no tongue, will speak
With most miraculous organ. I'll have these players
Play something like the murder of my father
Before mine uncle. I'll observe his looks,
I'll tent him to the quick. If 'a do blench,
I know my course. The spirit that I have seen
May be a devil, and the devil hath power
T' assume a pleasing shape, yea, and perhaps
Out of my weakness and my melancholy,
As he is very potent with such spirits,
Abuses me to damn me. I'll have grounds
More relative than this. The play's the thing
Wherein I'll catch the conscience of the King.

Be Classic.

COMING SOON FROM PUFFIN BOOKS

Dracula	Bram Stoker
Emma	Jane Austen
The Fall of the House of Usher & Other Stories	Edgar Allan Poe
Frankenstein	Mary Shelley
Jane Eyre	Charlotte Brontë
Pride and Prejudice	Jane Austen
Romeo and Juliet	William Shakespeare

The Tragedy of

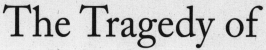

Prince of Denmark

William Shakespeare

PUFFIN BOOKS
An Imprint of Penguin Group (USA) Inc.

PUFFIN BOOKS
Published by the Penguin Group
Penguin Young Readers Group, 345 Hudson Street, New York, New York 10014, U.S.A.
Penguin Group (Canada), 90 Eglinton Avenue East, Suite 700, Toronto, Ontario, Canada M4P 2Y3
(a division of Pearson Penguin Canada Inc.)
Penguin Books Ltd, 80 Strand, London WC2R 0RL, England
Penguin Ireland, 25 St Stephen's Green, Dublin 2, Ireland (a division of Penguin Books Ltd)
Penguin Group (Australia), 250 Camberwell Road, Camberwell, Victoria 3124, Australia
(a division of Pearson Australia Group Pty Ltd)
Penguin Books India Pvt Ltd, 11 Community Centre, Panchsheel Park, New Delhi - 110 017, India
Penguin Group (NZ), 67 Apollo Drive, Rosedale, North Shore 0632, New Zealand
(a division of Pearson New Zealand Ltd.)
Penguin Books (South Africa) (Pty) Ltd, 24 Sturdee Avenue,
Rosebank, Johannesburg 2196, South Africa

Registered Offices: Penguin Books Ltd, 80 Strand, London WC2R 0RL, England

Published by Puffin Books, a division of Penguin Young Readers Group, 2011

1 3 5 7 9 10 8 6 4 2

Puffin ISBN 978-0-14-241917-5

Printed in the United States of America

The Tragedy of
HAMLET
Prince of Denmark

[*Dramatis Personae*

Hamlet, Prince of Denmark, son of the late king and of
   Gertrude
Claudius, King of Denmark, Hamlet's uncle
Ghost of the late king, Hamlet's father
Gertrude, Queen of Denmark, widow of the late king, now
   wife of Claudius
Polonius, councillor to the king
Laertes, son of Polonius
Ophelia, daughter of Polonius
Reynaldo, servant of Polonius
Horatio, Hamlet's friend and fellow student
Rosencrantz ⎫
Guildenstern ⎭ courtiers, former school friends of Hamlet
Voltemand ⎫
Cornelius ⎭ Danish ambassadors to Norway
Osric, a foppish courtier
Marcellus ⎫
Barnardo ⎬ soldiers
Francisco ⎭
English ambassadors
Fortinbras, prince of Norway
Captain, in Fortinbras's army
Players, performing the roles of Prologue, King, Queen,
   and Lucianus
A Priest
Two Clowns—a Grave-digger and his companion
Lords, Ladies, Soldiers, Sailors, Messengers, Attendants

Scene: In and around the court at Elsinore]

The Tragedy of Hamlet
Prince of Denmark

[ACT 1

Scene 1. *A guard platform of the castle.*]

Enter Barnardo and Francisco, two sentinels.

Barnardo. Who's there?

Francisco. Nay, answer me. Stand and unfold°¹ yourself.

Barnardo. Long live the King!°

Francisco. Barnardo?

Barnardo. He.   5

Francisco. You come most carefully upon your hour.

Barnardo. 'Tis now struck twelve. Get thee to bed,
Francisco.

---

¹The degree sign (°) indicates a footnote, which is keyed to the text by
the line number. Text references are printed in **boldface** type; the anno-
tation follows in roman type.
1.1.2 **unfold** disclose   3 **Long live the King** (perhaps a password, perhaps a greeting)

Francisco. For this relief much thanks. 'Tis bitter cold,
And I am sick at heart.

Barnardo. Have you had quiet guard?

10 *Francisco.*   Not a mouse stirring.

Barnardo. Well, good night.
If you do meet Horatio and Marcellus,
The rivals° of my watch, bid them make haste.

           Enter Horatio and Marcellus.

Francisco. I think I hear them. Stand, ho! Who is
there?

Horatio. Friends to this ground.

15 *Marcellus.*   And liegemen to the Dane.°

Francisco. Give you° good night.

Marcellus.   O, farewell, honest soldier.
Who hath relieved you?

Francisco.   Barnardo hath my place.
Give you good night.   *Exit Francisco.*

Marcellus.   Holla, Barnardo!

Barnardo.   Say——
What, is Horatio there?

Horatio.   A piece of him.

20 *Barnardo.* Welcome, Horatio. Welcome, good Marcellus.

Marcellus. What, has this thing appeared again tonight?

Barnardo. I have seen nothing.

Marcellus. Horatio says 'tis but our fantasy,
And will not let belief take hold of him
25 Touching this dreaded sight twice seen of us;
Therefore I have entreated him along
With us to watch the minutes of this night,
That, if again this apparition come,
He may approve° our eyes and speak to it.

---

13 **rivals** partners   15 **liegemen to the Dane** loyal subjects to the King
of Denmark   16 **Give you** God give you   29 **approve** confirm

Horatio. Tush, tush, 'twill not appear.

Barnardo.   Sit down awhile,   30
And let us once again assail your ears,
That are so fortified against our story,
What we have two nights seen.

Horatio.   Well, sit we down,
And let us hear Barnardo speak of this.

Barnardo. Last night of all,   35
When yond same star that's westward from the
   pole°
Had made his course t' illume that part of heaven
Where now it burns, Marcellus and myself,
The bell then beating one——

               Enter Ghost.

Marcellus. Peace, break thee off. Look where it comes
again.   40

Barnardo. In the same figure like the king that's dead.

Marcellus. Thou art a scholar; speak to it, Horatio.

Barnardo. Looks 'a not like the king? Mark it, Horatio.

Horatio. Most like: it harrows me with fear and wonder.

Barnardo. It would be spoke to.

Marcellus.   Speak to it, Horatio.   45

Horatio. What art thou that usurp'st this time of night,
Together with that fair and warlike form
In which the majesty of buried Denmark°
Did sometimes march? By heaven I charge thee,
speak.

Marcellus. It is offended.

Barnardo.   See, it stalks away.   50

Horatio. Stay! Speak, speak. I charge thee, speak.
                      Exit Ghost.

36 **pole** polestar   48 **buried Denmark** the buried King of Denmark

Marcellus. 'Tis gone and will not answer.

Barnardo. How now, Horatio? You tremble and look
    pale.
    Is not this something more than fantasy?
55   What think you on't?

Horatio. Before my God, I might not this believe
    Without the sensible and true avouch°
    Of mine own eyes.

Marcellus.   Is it not like the King?

Horatio. As thou art to thyself.
60   Such was the very armor he had on
    When he the ambitious Norway° combated:
    So frowned he once, when, in an angry parle,°
    He smote the sledded Polacks° on the ice.
    'Tis strange.

Marcellus. Thus twice before, and jump° at this dead
65   hour,
    With martial stalk hath he gone by our watch.

Horatio. In what particular thought to work I know
    not;
    But, in the gross and scope° of my opinion,
    This bodes some strange eruption to our state.

Marcellus. Good now, sit down, and tell me he that
70   knows,
    Why this same strict and most observant watch
    So nightly toils the subject° of the land,
    And why such daily cast of brazen cannon
    And foreign mart° for implements of war,

57 **sensible and true avouch** sensory and true proof   61 **Norway** King
of Norway   62 **parle** parley   63 **sledded Polacks** Poles in sledges
65 **jump** just   68 **gross and scope** general drift   72 **toils the subject**
makes the subjects toil   74 **mart** trading

Why such impress° of shipwrights, whose sore task   *75*
Does not divide the Sunday from the week,
What might be toward° that this sweaty haste
Doth make the night joint-laborer with the day?
Who is't that can inform me?

Horatio.   That can I.
  At least the whisper goes so: our last king,   *80*
  Whose image even but now appeared to us,
  Was, as you know, by Fortinbras of Norway,
  Thereto pricked on by a most emulate pride,
  Dared to the combat; in which our valiant Hamlet
  (For so this side of our known world esteemed him)   *85*
  Did slay this Fortinbras, who, by a sealed compact
  Well ratified by law and heraldry,°
  Did forfeit, with his life, all those his lands
  Which he stood seized° of, to the conqueror;
  Against the which a moiety competent°   *90*
  Was gagèd° by our King, which had returned
  To the inheritance of Fortinbras,
  Had he been vanquisher, as, by the same comart°
  And carriage of the article designed,°
  His fell to Hamlet. Now, sir, young Fortinbras,   *95*
  Of unimprovèd° mettle hot and full,
  Hath in the skirts° of Norway here and there
  Sharked up° a list of lawless resolutes,°
  For food and diet, to some enterprise
  That hath a stomach in't;° which is no other,   *100*
  As it doth well appear unto our state,
  But to recover of us by strong hand
  And terms compulsatory, those foresaid lands
  So by his father lost; and this, I take it,
  Is the main motive of our preparations,   *105*

---

75 impress forced service   **77 toward** in preparation   **87 law and heraldry** heraldic law (governing the combat)   **89 seized** possessed
90 moiety competent equal portion   **91 gagèd** engaged, pledged
93 comart agreement   **94 carriage of the article designed** import of
the agreement drawn up   **96 unimprovèd** untried   **97 skirts** borders
98 Sharked up collected indiscriminately (as a shark gulps its prey)
98 resolutes desperadoes   **100 hath a stomach in't** i.e., requires
courage

The source of this our watch, and the chief head°
Of this posthaste and romage° in the land.

Barnardo. I think it be no other but e'en so;
Well may it sort° that this portentous figure
110   Comes armèd through our watch so like the King
That was and is the question of these wars.

Horatio. A mote it is to trouble the mind's eye:
In the most high and palmy state of Rome,
A little ere the mightiest Julius fell,
115   The graves stood tenantless, and the sheeted dead
Did squeak and gibber in the Roman streets;°
As stars with trains of fire and dews of blood,
Disasters° in the sun; and the moist star,°
Upon whose influence Neptune's empire stands,
120   Was sick almost to doomsday with eclipse.
And even the like precurse° of feared events,
As harbingers° preceding still° the fates
And prologue to the omen° coming on,
Have heaven and earth together demonstrated
125   Unto our climatures° and countrymen.

Enter Ghost.

But soft, behold, lo where it comes again!
I'll cross it,° though it blast me.—Stay, illusion.

It spreads his° arms.

If thou hast any sound or use of voice,
Speak to me.
130   If there be any good thing to be done
That may to thee do ease and grace to me,
Speak to me.
If thou art privy to thy country's fate,
Which happily° foreknowing may avoid,

---

106 **head** fountainhead, origin   107 **romage** bustle   109 **sort** be-
fit   116 **Did squeak ... Roman streets** (the break in the sense which
follows this line suggests that a line has dropped out)   118 **Disasters**
threatening signs   118 **moist star** moon   121 **precurse** precursor, fore-
shadowing   122 **harbingers** forerunners   122 **still** always   123 **omen**
calamity   125 **climatures** regions   127 **cross it** (1) cross its path, confront it (2) make the sign of the cross in front of it   127 s.d. **his** i.e., its,
the ghost's (though possibly what is meant is that Horatio spreads his
own arms, making a cross of himself)   134 **happily** haply, perhaps

O, speak!   *135*
Or if thou hast uphoarded in thy life
Extorted° treasure in the womb of earth,
For which, they say, you spirits oft walk in death,
                              The cock crows.
Speak of it. Stay and speak. Stop it, Marcellus.

Marcellus. Shall I strike at it with my partisan?°   *140*

Horatio. Do, if it will not stand.

Barnardo.   'Tis here.

Horatio.   'Tis here.

Marcellus. 'Tis gone.   *Exit Ghost.*
We do it wrong, being so majestical,
To offer it the show of violence,
For it is as the air, invulnerable,   *145*
And our vain blows malicious mockery.

Barnardo. It was about to speak when the cock crew.

Horatio. And then it started, like a guilty thing
Upon a fearful summons. I have heard,
The cock, that is the trumpet to the morn,   *150*
Doth with his lofty and shrill-sounding throat
Awake the god of day, and at his warning,
Whether in sea or fire, in earth or air,
Th' extravagant and erring° spirit hies
To his confine; and of the truth herein   *155*
This present object made probation.°

Marcellus. It faded on the crowing of the cock.
Some say that ever 'gainst° that season comes
Wherein our Savior's birth is celebrated,
This bird of dawning singeth all night long,   *160*
And then, they say, no spirit dare stir abroad,
The nights are wholesome, then no planets strike,°
No fairy takes,° nor witch hath power to charm:
So hallowed and so gracious is that time.

Horatio. So have I heard and do in part believe it.   *165*

---

137 **Extorted** ill-won   140 **partisan** pike (a long-handled weapon)
154 **extravagant and erring** out of bounds and wandering   156 **probation** proof   158 **'gainst** just before   162 **strike** exert an evil influence
163 **takes** bewitches

But look, the morn in russet mantle clad
Walks o'er the dew of yon high eastward hill.
Break we our watch up, and by my advice
Let us impart what we have seen tonight
170   Unto young Hamlet, for upon my life
This spirit, dumb to us, will speak to him.
Do you consent we shall acquaint him with it,
As needful in our loves, fitting our duty?

Marcellus. Let's do't, I pray, and I this morning know
175   Where we shall find him most convenient.   *Exeunt.*

[Scene 2. *The castle.*]

*Flourish.° Enter Claudius, King of Denmark, Gertrude
the Queen, Councilors, Polonius and his son Laertes,
Hamlet, cum aliis° [including Voltemand and Cor-
nelius].*

King. Though yet of Hamlet our dear brother's death
The memory be green, and that it us befitted
To bear our hearts in grief, and our whole kingdom
To be contracted in one brow of woe,
5   Yet so far hath discretion fought with nature
That we with wisest sorrow think on him
Together with remembrance of ourselves.
Therefore our sometime sister,° now our Queen,
Th' imperial jointress° to this warlike state,
10   Have we, as 'twere, with a defeated joy,
With an auspicious° and a dropping eye,
With mirth in funeral, and with dirge in marriage,
In equal scale weighing delight and dole,
Taken to wife. Nor have we herein barred
15   Your better wisdoms, which have freely gone

1.2.s.d. **Flourish** fanfare of trumpets   s.d. **cum aliis** with others (Latin)
8 **our sometime sister** my (the royal "we") former sister-in-law
9 **jointress** joint tenant, partner   11 **auspicious** joyful

With this affair along. For all, our thanks.
Now follows that you know young Fortinbras,
Holding a weak supposal of our worth,
Or thinking by our late dear brother's death
Our state to be disjoint and out of frame,°   20
Colleaguèd with this dream of his advantage,°
He hath not failed to pester us with message,
Importing the surrender of those lands
Lost by his father, with all bands of law,
To our most valiant brother. So much for him.   25
Now for ourself and for this time of meeting.
Thus much the business is: we have here writ
To Norway, uncle of young Fortinbras—
Who, impotent and bedrid, scarcely hears
Of this his nephew's purpose—to suppress   30
His further gait° herein, in that the levies,
The lists, and full proportions° are all made
Out of his subject;° and we here dispatch
You, good Cornelius, and you, Voltemand,
For bearers of this greeting to old Norway,   35
Giving to you no further personal power
To business with the King, more than the scope
Of these delated articles° allow.
Farewell, and let your haste commend your duty.

Cornelius, Voltemand. In that, and all things, will we
    show our duty.   40

King. We doubt it nothing. Heartily farewell.
                        Exit Voltemand and Cornelius.
And now, Laertes, what's the news with you?
You told us of some suit. What is't, Laertes?
You cannot speak of reason to the Dane
And lose your voice.° What wouldst thou beg,
    Laertes,   45
That shall not be my offer, not thy asking?
The head is not more native° to the heart,

20 **frame** order   21 **advantage** superiority   31 **gait** proceeding   32 **proportions** supplies for war   33 **Out of his subject** i.e., out of old Norway's subjects and realm   38 **delated articles** detailed documents   45 **lose your voice** waste your breath   47 **native** related

The hand more instrumental to the mouth,
Than is the throne of Denmark to thy father.
What wouldst thou have, Laertes?

50 *Laertes.*   My dread lord,
Your leave and favor to return to France,
From whence, though willingly I came to Denmark
To show my duty in your coronation,
Yet now I must confess, that duty done,
55 My thoughts and wishes bend again toward France
And bow them to your gracious leave and pardon.

King. Have you your father's leave? What says Polonius?

Polonius. He hath, my lord, wrung from me my slow
leave
By laborsome petition, and at last
60 Upon his will I sealed my hard consent.°
I do beseech you give him leave to go.

King. Take thy fair hour, Laertes. Time be thine,
And thy best graces spend it at thy will.
But now, my cousin° Hamlet, and my son——

Hamlet. [*Aside*] A little more than kin, and less than
65 kind!°

King. How is it that the clouds still hang on you?

Hamlet. Not so, my lord. I am too much in the sun.°

Queen. Good Hamlet, cast thy nighted color off,
And let thine eye look like a friend on Denmark.
70 Do not forever with thy vailèd° lids
Seek for thy noble father in the dust.
Thou know'st 'tis common; all that lives must die,
Passing through nature to eternity.

60 **Upon his ... hard consent** to his desire I gave my reluctant
consent   64 **cousin** kinsman   65 **kind** (pun on the meanings "kindly"
and "natural"; though doubly related—**more than kin**—Hamlet asserts
that he neither resembles Claudius in nature nor feels kindly toward
him)   67 **sun** sunshine of royal favor (with a pun on "son")   70 **vailèd**
lowered

Hamlet. Ay, madam, it is common.°

Queen.   If it be,
  Why seems it so particular with thee?   75

Hamlet. Seems, madam? Nay, it is. I know not "seems."
  'Tis not alone my inky cloak, good mother,
  Nor customary suits of solemn black,
  Nor windy suspiration° of forced breath,
  No, nor the fruitful river in the eye,   80
  Nor the dejected havior of the visage,
  Together with all forms, moods, shapes of grief,
  That can denote me truly. These indeed seem,
  For they are actions that a man might play,
  But I have that within which passes show;   85
  These but the trappings and the suits of woe.

King. 'Tis sweet and commendable in your nature,
    Hamlet,
  To give these mourning duties to your father,
  But you must know your father lost a father,
  That father lost, lost his, and the survivor bound   90
  In filial obligation for some term
  To do obsequious° sorrow. But to persever
  In obstinate condolement° is a course
  Of impious stubbornness. 'Tis unmanly grief.
  It shows a will most incorrect to heaven,   95
  A heart unfortified, a mind impatient,
  An understanding simple and unschooled.
  For what we know must be and is as common
  As any the most vulgar° thing to sense,
  Why should we in our peevish opposition   100
  Take it to heart? Fie, 'tis a fault to heaven,
  A fault against the dead, a fault to nature,
  To reason most absurd, whose common theme
  Is death of fathers, and who still hath cried,
  From the first corse° till he that died today,   105
  "This must be so." We pray you throw to earth

74 **common** (1) universal (2) vulgar   79 **windy suspiration** heavy sighing   92 **obsequious** suitable to obsequies (funerals)   93 **condolement**
mourning   99 **vulgar** common   105 **corse** corpse

This unprevailing° woe, and think of us
As of a father, for let the world take note
You are the most immediate to our throne,
110 And with no less nobility of love
Than that which dearest father bears his son
Do I impart toward you. For your intent
In going back to school in Wittenberg,
It is most retrograde° to our desire,
115 And we beseech you, bend you° to remain
Here in the cheer and comfort of our eye,
Our chiefest courtier, cousin, and our son.

Queen. Let not thy mother lose her prayers, Hamlet.
I pray thee stay with us, go not to Wittenberg.

120 *Hamlet.* I shall in all my best obey you, madam.

King. Why, 'tis a loving and a fair reply.
Be as ourself in Denmark. Madam, come.
This gentle and unforced accord of Hamlet
Sits smiling to my heart, in grace whereof
125 No jocund health that Denmark drinks today,
But the great cannon to the clouds shall tell,
And the King's rouse° the heaven shall bruit° again,
Respeaking earthly thunder. Come away.
                 Flourish. Exeunt all but Hamlet.

Hamlet. O that this too too sullied° flesh would melt,
130 Thaw, and resolve itself into a dew,
Or that the Everlasting had not fixed
His canon° 'gainst self-slaughter. O God, God,
How weary, stale, flat, and unprofitable
Seem to me all the uses of this world!
135 Fie on't, ah, fie, 'tis an unweeded garden
That grows to seed. Things rank and gross in nature
Possess it merely.° That it should come to this:
But two months dead, nay, not so much, not two,

---

107 **unprevailing** unavailing 114 **retrograde** contrary 115 **bend
you** incline 127 **rouse** deep drink 127 **bruit** announce noisily
129 **sullied** (Q2 has **sallied,** here modernized to **sullied,** which makes
sense and is therefore given; but the Folio reading, **solid,** which fits better with **melt,** is quite possibly correct) 132 **canon** law 137 **merely**
entirely

So excellent a king, that was to this
Hyperion° to a satyr, so loving to my mother   *140*
That he might not beteem° the winds of heaven
Visit her face too roughly. Heaven and earth,
Must I remember? Why, she would hang on him
As if increase of appetite had grown
By what it fed on; and yet within a month—   *145*
Let me not think on't; frailty, thy name is woman—
A little month, or ere those shoes were old
With which she followed my poor father's body
Like Niobe,° all tears, why, she—
O God, a beast that wants discourse of reason°   *150*
Would have mourned longer—married with my
    uncle,
My father's brother, but no more like my father
Than I to Hercules. Within a month,
Ere yet the salt of most unrighteous tears
Had left the flushing° in her gallèd eyes,   *155*
She married. O, most wicked speed, to post°
With such dexterity to incestuous° sheets!
It is not, nor it cannot come to good.
But break my heart, for I must hold my tongue.

   Enter Horatio, Marcellus, and Barnardo.

Horatio. Hail to your lordship!

Hamlet.   I am glad to see you well.   *160*
    Horatio—or I do forget myself.

Horatio. The same, my lord, and your poor servant
    ever.

Hamlet. Sir, my good friend, I'll change° that name
    with you.
    And what make you from Wittenberg, Horatio?
    Marcellus.   *165*

140 **Hyperion** the sun god, a model of beauty   141 **beteem** allow
149 **Niobe** (a mother who wept profusely at the death of her children)
150 **wants discourse of reason** lacks reasoning power   155 **left the
flushing** stopped reddening   156 **post** hasten   157 **incestuous** (canon
law considered marriage with a deceased brother's widow to be incestuous)   163 **change** exchange

Marcellus. My good lord!

Hamlet. I am very glad to see you. [*To Barnardo*]
  Good even, sir.
  But what, in faith, make you from Wittenberg?

Horatio. A truant disposition, good my lord.

170 *Hamlet.* I would not hear your enemy say so,
  Nor shall you do my ear that violence
  To make it truster° of your own report
  Against yourself. I know you are no truant.
  But what is your affair in Elsinore?
175   We'll teach you to drink deep ere you depart.

Horatio. My lord, I came to see your father's funeral.

Hamlet. I prithee do not mock me, fellow student.
  I think it was to see my mother's wedding.

Horatio. Indeed, my lord, it followed hard upon.

180 *Hamlet.* Thrift, thrift, Horatio. The funeral baked
  meats
  Did coldly furnish forth the marriage tables.
  Would I had met my dearest° foe in heaven
  Or ever I had seen that day, Horatio!
  My father, methinks I see my father.

Horatio. Where, my lord?

185 *Hamlet.*   In my mind's eye, Horatio.

Horatio. I saw him once. 'A° was a goodly king.

Hamlet. 'A was a man, take him for all in all,
  I shall not look upon his like again.

Horatio. My lord, I think I saw him yesternight.

190 *Hamlet.* Saw? Who?

Horatio. My lord, the King your father.

Hamlet.   The King my father?

Horatio. Season your admiration° for a while
  With an attent ear till I may deliver
  Upon the witness of these gentlemen

172 **truster** believer 182 **dearest** most intensely felt 186 **'A** he
192 **Season your admiration** control your wonder

This marvel to you.

Hamlet.   For God's love let me hear!   *195*

Horatio. Two nights together had these gentlemen,
  Marcellus and Barnardo, on their watch
  In the dead waste and middle of the night
  Been thus encountered. A figure like your father,
  Armèd at point exactly, cap-a-pe,°   *200*
  Appears before them, and with solemn march
  Goes slow and stately by them. Thrice he walked
  By their oppressed and fear-surprisèd eyes,
  Within his truncheon's length,° whilst they, distilled°
  Almost to jelly with the act° of fear,   *205*
  Stand dumb and speak not to him. This to me
  In dreadful° secrecy impart they did,
  And I with them the third night kept the watch,
  Where, as they had delivered, both in time,
  Form of the thing, each word made true and good,   *210*
  The apparition comes. I knew your father.
  These hands are not more like.

Hamlet.   But where was this?

Marcellus. My lord, upon the platform where we
  watched.

Hamlet. Did you not speak to it?

Horatio.   My lord, I did;
  But answer made it none. Yet once methought   *215*
  It lifted up it° head and did address
  Itself to motion like as it would speak:
  But even then the morning cock crew loud,
  And at the sound it shrunk in haste away
  And vanished from our sight.

Hamlet.   'Tis very strange.   *220*

Horatio. As I do live, my honored lord, 'tis true,
  And we did think it writ down in our duty
  To let you know of it.

200 **cap-a-pe** head to foot   204 **truncheon's length** space of a short
staff   204 **distilled** reduced   205 **act** action   207 **dreadful** terrified
216 **it** its

Hamlet. Indeed, indeed, sirs, but this troubles me.
   Hold you the watch tonight?

225 *All.*   We do, my lord.

Hamlet. Armed, say you?

All. Armed, my lord.

Hamlet. From top to toe?

All.   My lord, from head to foot.

Hamlet. Then saw you not his face.

230 *Horatio.* O, yes, my lord. He wore his beaver° up.

Hamlet. What, looked he frowningly?

Horatio. A countenance more in sorrow than in anger.

Hamlet. Pale or red?

Horatio. Nay, very pale.

Hamlet.   And fixed his eyes upon you?

Horatio. Most constantly.

235 *Hamlet.*   I would I had been there.

Horatio. It would have much amazed you.

Hamlet. Very like, very like. Stayed it long?

Horatio. While one with moderate haste might tell° a
   hundred.

Both. Longer, longer.

Horatio. Not when I saw't.

240 *Hamlet.*   His beard was grizzled,° no?

Horatio. It was as I have seen it in his life,
   A sable silvered.°

Hamlet.   I will watch tonight.
   Perchance 'twill walk again.

Horatio.   I warr'nt it will.

Hamlet. If it assume my noble father's person,

230 **beaver** visor, face guard   238 **tell** count   240 **grizzled** gray
242 **sable silvered** black mingled with white

I'll speak to it though hell itself should gape   *245*
And bid me hold my peace. I pray you all,
If you have hitherto concealed this sight,
Let it be tenable° in your silence still,
And whatsomever else shall hap tonight,
Give it an understanding but no tongue;   *250*
I will requite your loves. So fare you well.
Upon the platform 'twixt eleven and twelve
I'll visit you.

All.   Our duty to your honor.

Hamlet. Your loves, as mine to you. Farewell.
                              Exeunt [all but Hamlet].
My father's spirit—in arms? All is not well.   *255*
I doubt° some foul play. Would the night were come!
Till then sit still, my soul. Foul deeds will rise,
Though all the earth o'erwhelm them, to men's eyes.
                                              Exit.

[Scene 3. *A room.*]

Enter Laertes and Ophelia, his sister.

Laertes. My necessaries are embarked. Farewell.
    And, sister, as the winds give benefit
    And convoy° is assistant, do not sleep,
    But let me hear from you.

Ophelia.   Do you doubt that?

Laertes. For Hamlet, and the trifling of his favor,   *5*
    Hold it a fashion and a toy° in blood,
    A violet in the youth of primy° nature,
    Forward,° not permanent, sweet, not lasting,
    The perfume and suppliance° of a minute,

248 **tenable** held   256 **doubt** suspect   1.3.3 **convoy** conveyance   6 **toy**
idle fancy   7 **primy** springlike   8 **Forward** premature   9 **suppliance**
diversion

No more.

Ophelia.   No more but so?

10   *Laertes.*   Think it no more.
        For nature crescent° does not grow alone
        In thews° and bulk, but as this temple° waxes,
        The inward service of the mind and soul
        Grows wide withal. Perhaps he loves you now,
15   And now no soil nor cautel° doth besmirch
        The virtue of his will; but you must fear,
        His greatness weighed,° his will is not his own.
        For he himself is subject to his birth.
        He may not, as unvalued° persons do,
20   Carve for himself; for on his choice depends
        The safety and health of this whole state;
        And therefore must his choice be circumscribed
        Unto the voice and yielding of that body
        Whereof he is the head. Then if he says he loves you,
25   It fits your wisdom so far to believe it
        As he in his particular act and place
        May give his saying deed, which is no further
        Than the main voice of Denmark goes withal.
        Then weigh what loss your honor may sustain
30   If with too credent° ear you list his songs,
        Or lose your heart, or your chaste treasure open
        To his unmastered importunity.
        Fear it, Ophelia, fear it, my dear sister,
        And keep you in the rear of your affection,
35   Out of the shot and danger of desire.
        The chariest maid is prodigal enough
        If she unmask her beauty to the moon.
        Virtue itself scapes not calumnious strokes.
        The canker° galls the infants of the spring
40   Too oft before their buttons° be disclosed,
        And in the morn and liquid dew of youth
        Contagious blastments are most imminent.

11 **crescent** growing   12 **thews** muscles and sinews   12 **temple** i.e.,
the body   15 **cautel** deceit   17 **greatness weighed** high rank considered   19 **unvalued** of low rank   30 **credent** credulous   39 **canker**
cankerworm   40 **buttons** buds

Be wary then; best safety lies in fear;
Youth to itself rebels, though none else near.

Ophelia. I shall the effect of this good lesson keep   *45*
As watchman to my heart, but, good my brother,
Do not, as some ungracious° pastors do,
Show me the steep and thorny way to heaven,
Whiles, like a puffed and reckless libertine,
Himself the primrose path of dalliance treads   *50*
And recks not his own rede.°

Enter Polonius.

Laertes.   O, fear me not.
I stay too long. But here my father comes.
A double blessing is a double grace;
Occasion smiles upon a second leave.

Polonius. Yet here, Laertes? Aboard, aboard, for
    shame!   *55*
The wind sits in the shoulder of your sail,
And you are stayed for. There—my blessing with
    thee,
And these few precepts in thy memory
Look thou character.° Give thy thoughts no tongue,
Nor any unproportioned° thought his act.   *60*
Be thou familiar, but by no means vulgar.
Those friends thou hast, and their adoption tried,
Grapple them unto thy soul with hoops of steel,
But do not dull thy palm with entertainment
Of each new-hatched, unfledged courage.° Beware   *65*
Of entrance to a quarrel; but being in,
Bear't that th' opposèd may beware of thee.
Give every man thine ear, but few thy voice;
Take each man's censure,° but reserve thy judgment.
Costly thy habit as thy purse can buy,   *70*
But not expressed in fancy; rich, not gaudy,
For the apparel oft proclaims the man,
And they in France of the best rank and station

---

47 **ungracious** lacking grace   51 **recks not his own rede** does not heed
his own advice   59 **character** inscribe   60 **unproportioned** unbal-
anced   65 **courage** gallant youth   69 **censure** opinion

Are of a most select and generous, chief in that.°
75 Neither a borrower nor a lender be,
For loan oft loses both itself and friend,
And borrowing dulleth edge of husbandry.°
This above all, to thine own self be true,
And it must follow, as the night the day,
80 Thou canst not then be false to any man.
Farewell. My blessing season this° in thee!

Laertes. Most humbly do I take my leave, my lord.

Polonius. The time invites you. Go, your servants
tend.°

Laertes. Farewell, Ophelia, and remember well
What I have said to you.

85 *Ophelia.*   'Tis in my memory locked,
And you yourself shall keep the key of it.

Laertes. Farewell.   *Exit Laertes.*

Polonius. What is't, Ophelia, he hath said to you?

Ophelia. So please you, something touching the Lord
Hamlet.

90 *Polonius.* Marry,° well bethought.
'Tis told me he hath very oft of late
Given private time to you, and you yourself
Have of your audience been most free and bounte-
ous.
If it be so—as so 'tis put on me,
95 And that in way of caution—I must tell you
You do not understand yourself so clearly
As it behooves my daughter and your honor.
What is between you? Give me up the truth.

Ophelia. He hath, my lord, of late made many tenders°
100 Of his affection to me.

---

74 **Are of . . . in that** show their fine taste and their gentlemanly in-
stincts more in that than in any other point of manners (Kittredge)
77 **husbandry** thrift 81 **season this** make fruitful this (advice)
83 **tend** attend 90 **Marry** (a light oath, from "By the Virgin Mary")
99 **tenders** offers (in line 103 it has the same meaning, but in line 106
Polonius speaks of **tenders** in the sense of counters or chips; in line
109 **Tend'ring** means "holding," and **tender** means "give," "present")

Polonius. Affection pooh! You speak like a green girl,
    Unsifted° in such perilous circumstance.
    Do you believe his tenders, as you call them?

Ophelia. I do not know, my lord, what I should think.

Polonius. Marry, I will teach you. Think yourself a
    baby   *105*
    That you have ta'en these tenders for true pay
    Which are not sterling. Tender yourself more dearly,
    Or (not to crack the wind of the poor phrase)
    Tend'ring it thus you'll tender me a fool.°

Ophelia. My lord, he hath importuned me with love   *110*
    In honorable fashion.

Polonius. Ay, fashion you may call it. Go to, go to.

Ophelia. And hath given countenance to his speech, my
    lord,
    With almost all the holy vows of heaven.

Polonius. Ay, springes to catch woodcocks.° I do know,   *115*
    When the blood burns, how prodigal the soul
    Lends the tongue vows. These blazes, daughter,
    Giving more light than heat, extinct in both,
    Even in their promise, as it is a-making,
    You must not take for fire. From this time   *120*
    Be something scanter of your maiden presence.
    Set your entreatments° at a higher rate
    Than a command to parley. For Lord Hamlet,
    Believe so much in him that he is young,
    And with a larger tether may he walk   *125*
    Than may be given you. In few, Ophelia,
    Do not believe his vows, for they are brokers,°
    Not of that dye° which their investments° show,
    But mere implorators° of unholy suits,
    Breathing like sanctified and pious bonds,°   *130*
    The better to beguile. This is for all:

102 **Unsifted** untried   109 **tender me a fool** (1) present me with a fool
(2) present me with a baby   115 **springes to catch woodcocks** snares to
catch stupid birds   122 **entreatments** interviews   127 **brokers** procur-
ers   128 **dye** i.e., kind   128 **investments** garments   129 **implorators**
solicitors   130 **bonds** pledges

I would not, in plain terms, from this time forth
Have you so slander° any moment leisure
As to give words or talk with the Lord Hamlet.
135   Look to't, I charge you. Come your ways.

Ophelia. I shall obey, my lord.   *Exeunt.*

[Scene 4. *A guard platform.*]

Enter Hamlet, Horatio, and Marcellus.

Hamlet. The air bites shrewdly;° it is very cold.

Horatio. It is a nipping and an eager° air.

Hamlet. What hour now?

Horatio.   I think it lacks of twelve.

Marcellus. No, it is struck.

Horatio. Indeed? I heard it not. It then draws near the
5   season
Wherein the spirit held his wont to walk.
          A flourish of trumpets, and two pieces go off.
What does this mean, my lord?

Hamlet. The King doth wake° tonight and takes his
          rouse,°
Keeps wassail, and the swagg'ring upspring° reels,
10   And as he drains his draughts of Rhenish° down
The kettledrum and trumpet thus bray out
The triumph of his pledge.°

Horatio.   Is it a custom?

133 **slander** disgrace 1.4.1 **shrewdly** bitterly   2 **eager** sharp   8 **wake**
hold a revel by night   8 **takes his rouse** carouses   9 **upspring** (a
dance)   10 **Rhenish** Rhine wine   12 **The triumph of his pledge** the
achievement (of drinking a wine cup in one draught) of his toast

Hamlet. Ay, marry, is't,
   But to my mind, though I am native here
   And to the manner born, it is a custom   *15*
   More honored in the breach than the observance.
   This heavy-headed revel east and west
   Makes us traduced and taxed of° other nations.
   They clepe° us drunkards and with swinish phrase
   Soil our addition,° and indeed it takes   *20*
   From our achievements, though performed at height,
   The pith and marrow of our attribute.°
   So oft it chances in particular men
   That for some vicious mole° of nature in them,
   As in their birth, wherein they are not guilty,   *25*
   (Since nature cannot choose his origin)
   By the o'ergrowth of some complexion,°
   Oft breaking down the pales° and forts of reason,
   Or by some habit that too much o'erleavens°
   The form of plausive° manners, that (these men,   *30*
   Carrying, I say, the stamp of one defect,
   Being nature's livery, or fortune's star°)
   Their virtues else, be they as pure as grace,
   As infinite as man may undergo,
   Shall in the general censure° take corruption   *35*
   From that particular fault. The dram of evil
   Doth all the noble substance of a doubt,
   To his own scandal.°

Enter Ghost.

Horatio.   Look, my lord, it comes.

Hamlet. Angels and ministers of grace defend us!
   Be thou a spirit of health° or goblin damned,   *40*
   Bring with thee airs from heaven or blasts from hell,
   Be thy intents wicked or charitable,

18 **taxed of** blamed by   19 **clepe** call   20 **addition** reputation (literally, "title of honor")   22 **attribute** reputation   24 **mole** blemish   27 **complexion** natural disposition   28 **pales** enclosures   29 **o'erleavens** mixes with, corrupts   30 **plausive** pleasing   32 **nature's livery, or fortune's star** nature's equipment (i.e., "innate"), or a person's destiny determined by the stars   35 **general censure** popular judgment   36–38 **The dram . . . own scandal** (though the drift is clear, there is no agreement as to the exact meaning of these lines)   40 **spirit of health** good spirit

Thou com'st in such a questionable° shape
That I will speak to thee. I'll call thee Hamlet,
45   King, father, royal Dane. O, answer me!
Let me not burst in ignorance, but tell
Why thy canonized° bones, hearsèd in death,
Have burst their cerements,° why the sepulcher
Wherein we saw thee quietly interred
50   Hath oped his ponderous and marble jaws
To cast thee up again. What may this mean
That thou, dead corse, again in complete steel,
Revisits thus the glimpses of the moon,
Making night hideous, and we fools of nature
55   So horridly to shake our disposition°
With thoughts beyond the reaches of our souls?
Say, why is this? Wherefore? What should we do?
                         Ghost beckons Hamlet.

Horatio. It beckons you to go away with it,
  As if it some impartment° did desire
  To you alone.

60 *Marcellus.*   Look with what courteous action
  It waves you to a more removèd ground.
  But do not go with it.

Horatio.   No, by no means.

Hamlet. It will not speak. Then I will follow it.

Horatio. Do not, my lord.

Hamlet.   Why, what should be the fear?
65 I do not set my life at a pin's fee,
And for my soul, what can it do to that,
Being a thing immortal as itself?
It waves me forth again. I'll follow it.

Horatio. What if it tempt you toward the flood, my
  lord,
70 Or to the dreadful summit of the cliff

43 **questionable** (1) capable of discourse (2) dubious 47 **canonized** buried according to the canon or ordinance of the church 48 **cerements** waxed linen shroud 55 **shake our disposition** disturb us 59 **impartment** communication

That beetles° o'er his base into the sea,
And there assume some other horrible form,
Which might deprive your sovereignty of reason°
And draw you into madness? Think of it.
The very place puts toys° of desperation,   75
Without more motive, into every brain
That looks so many fathoms to the sea
And hears it roar beneath.

Hamlet.   It waves me still.
Go on; I'll follow thee.

Marcellus. You shall not go, my lord.

Hamlet.   Hold off your hands.   80

Horatio. Be ruled. You shall not go.

Hamlet.   My fate cries out
And makes each petty artere° in this body
As hardy as the Nemean lion's nerve.°
Still am I called! Unhand me, gentlemen.
By heaven, I'll make a ghost of him that lets° me!   85
I say, away! Go on. I'll follow thee.
                 Exit Ghost, and Hamlet.

Horatio. He waxes desperate with imagination.

Marcellus. Let's follow. 'Tis not fit thus to obey him.

Horatio. Have after! To what issue will this come?

Marcellus. Something is rotten in the state of Denmark.   90

Horatio. Heaven will direct it.

Marcellus.   Nay, let's follow him.   *Exeunt.*

71 **beetles** juts out   73 **deprive your sovereignty of reason** destroy the
sovereignty of your reason   75 **toys** whims, fancies   82 **artere** artery
83 **Nemean lion's nerve** sinews of the mythical lion slain by Hercules
85 **lets** hinders

[Scene 5. *The battlements.*]

Enter Ghost and Hamlet.

Hamlet. Whither wilt thou lead me? Speak; I'll go no
further.

Ghost. Mark me.

Hamlet.   I will.

Ghost.   My hour is almost come,
When I to sulf'rous and tormenting flames
Must render up myself.

Hamlet.   Alas, poor ghost.

5   *Ghost.* Pity me not, but lend thy serious hearing
To what I shall unfold.

Hamlet.   Speak. I am bound to hear.

Ghost. So art thou to revenge, when thou shalt hear.

Hamlet. What?

Ghost. I am thy father's spirit,
10   Doomed for a certain term to walk the night,
And for the day confined to fast in fires,
Till the foul crimes° done in my days of nature
Are burnt and purged away. But that I am forbid
To tell the secrets of my prison house,
15   I could a tale unfold whose lightest word
Would harrow up thy soul, freeze thy young blood,
Make thy two eyes like stars start from their
spheres,°
Thy knotted and combinèd locks to part,
And each particular hair to stand an end

1.5.12 **crimes** sins   17 **spheres** (in Ptolemaic astronomy, each planet
was fixed in a hollow transparent shell concentric with the earth)

Like quills upon the fearful porpentine.°   20
But this eternal blazon° must not be
To ears of flesh and blood. List, list, O, list!
If thou didst ever thy dear father love——

Hamlet. O God!

Ghost. Revenge his foul and most unnatural murder.   25

Hamlet. Murder?

Ghost. Murder most foul, as in the best it is,
But this most foul, strange, and unnatural.

Hamlet. Haste me to know't, that I, with wings as swift
As meditation° or the thoughts of love,   30
May sweep to my revenge.

Ghost.   I find thee apt,
And duller shouldst thou be than the fat weed
That roots itself in ease on Lethe wharf,°
Wouldst thou not stir in this. Now, Hamlet, hear.
'Tis given out that, sleeping in my orchard,   35
A serpent stung me. So the whole ear of Denmark
Is by a forgèd process° of my death
Rankly abused. But know, thou noble youth,
The serpent that did sting thy father's life
Now wears his crown.

Hamlet.   O my prophetic soul!   40
My uncle?

Ghost. Ay, that incestuous, that adulterate° beast,
With witchcraft of his wits, with traitorous gifts—
O wicked wit and gifts, that have the power
So to seduce!—won to his shameful lust   45
The will of my most seeming-virtuous queen.
O Hamlet, what a falling-off was there,
From me, whose love was of that dignity
That it went hand in hand even with the vow
I made to her in marriage, and to decline   50

20 **fearful porpentine** timid porcupine   21 **eternal blazon** revelation
of eternity   30 **meditation** thought   33 **Lethe wharf** bank of the river
of forgetfulness in Hades   37 **forgèd process** false account   42 **adulter-
ate** adulterous

Upon a wretch whose natural gifts were poor
To those of mine.
But virtue, as it never will be moved,
Though lewdness° court it in a shape of heaven,
55   So lust, though to a radiant angel linked,
Will sate itself in a celestial bed
And prey on garbage.
But soft, methinks I scent the morning air;
Brief let me be. Sleeping within my orchard,
60   My custom always of the afternoon,
Upon my secure° hour thy uncle stole
With juice of cursed hebona° in a vial,
And in the porches of my ears did pour
The leperous distillment, whose effect
65   Holds such an enmity with blood of man
That swift as quicksilver it courses through
The natural gates and alleys of the body,
And with a sudden vigor it doth posset°
And curd, like eager° droppings into milk,
70   The thin and wholesome blood. So did it mine,
And a most instant tetter° barked about
Most lazarlike° with vile and loathsome crust
All my smooth body.
Thus was I, sleeping, by a brother's hand
75   Of life, of crown, of queen at once dispatched,
Cut off even in the blossoms of my sin,
Unhouseled, disappointed, unaneled,°
No reck'ning made, but sent to my account
With all my imperfections on my head.
80   O, horrible! O, horrible! Most horrible!
If thou hast nature in thee, bear it not.
Let not the royal bed of Denmark be
A couch for luxury° and damnèd incest.
But howsomever thou pursues this act,
85   Taint not thy mind, nor let thy soul contrive

54 **lewdness** lust 61 **secure** unsuspecting 62 **hebona** a poisonous plant 68 **posset** curdle 69 **eager** acid 71 **tetter** scab 72 **lazarlike** leperlike 77 **Unhouseled, disappointed, unaneled** without the sacrament of communion, unabsolved, without extreme unction 83 **luxury** lust

Against thy mother aught. Leave her to heaven
And to those thorns that in her bosom lodge
To prick and sting her. Fare thee well at once.
The glowworm shows the matin° to be near
And 'gins to pale his uneffectual fire.   *90*
Adieu, adieu, adieu. Remember me.   *Exit.*

Hamlet. O all you host of heaven! O earth! What else?
And shall I couple hell? O fie! Hold, hold, my heart,
And you, my sinews, grow not instant old,
But bear me stiffly up. Remember thee?   *95*
Ay, thou poor ghost, whiles memory holds a seat
In this distracted globe.° Remember thee?
Yea, from the table° of my memory
I'll wipe away all trivial fond° records,
All saws° of books, all forms, all pressures° past   *100*
That youth and observation copied there,
And thy commandment all alone shall live
Within the book and volume of my brain,
Unmixed with baser matter. Yes, by heaven!
O most pernicious woman!   *105*
O villain, villain, smiling, damnèd villain!
My tables—meet it is I set it down
That one may smile, and smile, and be a villain.
At least I am sure it may be so in Denmark. [*Writes.*]
So, uncle, there you are. Now to my word: *110*
It is "Adieu, adieu, remember me."
I have sworn't.

Horatio and Marcellus. (*Within*) My lord, my lord!

              Enter Horatio and Marcellus.

Marcellus.   Lord Hamlet!

Horatio.   Heavens secure him!

Hamlet. So be it!

Marcellus. Illo, ho, ho,° my lord!   *115*

Hamlet. Hillo, ho, ho, boy! Come, bird, come.

89 **matin** morning   97 **globe** i.e., his head   98 **table** tablet, notebook
99 **fond** foolish   100 **saws** maxims   100 **pressures** impressions   115 **Illo,
ho, ho** (falconer's call to his hawk)

Marcellus. How is't, my noble lord?

Horatio.   What news, my lord?

Hamlet. O, wonderful!

Horatio. Good my lord, tell it.

Hamlet.   No, you will reveal it.

Horatio. Not I, my lord, by heaven.

120 *Marcellus.*   Nor I, my lord.

Hamlet. How say you then? Would heart of man once
    think it?
    But you'll be secret?

Both.   Ay, by heaven, my lord.

Hamlet. There's never a villain dwelling in all Denmark
    But he's an arrant knave.

Horatio. There needs no ghost, my lord, come from the
125   grave
    To tell us this.

Hamlet.   Why, right, you are in the right;
    And so, without more circumstance° at all,
    I hold it fit that we shake hands and part:
    You, as your business and desire shall point you,
130   For every man hath business and desire
    Such as it is, and for my own poor part,
    Look you, I'll go pray.

Horatio. These are but wild and whirling words, my
    lord.

Hamlet. I am sorry they offend you, heartily;
    Yes, faith, heartily.

135 *Horatio.*   There's no offense, my lord.

Hamlet. Yes, by Saint Patrick, but there is, Horatio,
    And much offense too. Touching this vision here,
    It is an honest ghost,° that let me tell you.
    For your desire to know what is between us,
140   O'ermaster't as you may. And now, good friends,

127 **circumstance** details   138 **honest ghost** i.e., not a demon in his father's shape

As you are friends, scholars, and soldiers,
Give me one poor request.

Horatio. What is't, my lord? We will.

Hamlet. Never make known what you have seen tonight.

Both. My lord, we will not.

Hamlet.   Nay, but swear't.

Horatio.   In faith,   *145*
My lord, not I.

Marcellus.   Nor I, my lord—in faith.

Hamlet. Upon my sword.

Marcellus.   We have sworn, my lord, already.

Hamlet. Indeed, upon my sword, indeed.
                   Ghost cries under the stage.

Ghost. Swear.

Hamlet. Ha, ha, boy, say'st thou so? Art thou there,
truepenny?°   *150*
Come on. You hear this fellow in the cellarage.
Consent to swear.

Horatio.   Propose the oath, my lord.

Hamlet. Never to speak of this that you have seen.
Swear by my sword.

Ghost. [*Beneath*] Swear.   *155*

Hamlet. Hic et ubique?° Then we'll shift our ground;
Come hither, gentlemen,
And lay your hands again upon my sword.
Swear by my sword
Never to speak of this that you have heard.   *160*

Ghost. [*Beneath*] Swear by his sword.

Hamlet. Well said, old mole! Canst work i' th' earth so
fast?
A worthy pioner!° Once more remove, good friends.

150 **truepenny** honest fellow   156 **Hic et ubique** here and everywhere
(Latin)   163 **pioner** digger of mines

Horatio. O day and night, but this is wondrous strange!

165 *Hamlet.* And therefore as a stranger give it welcome.
There are more things in heaven and earth, Horatio,
Than are dreamt of in your philosophy.
But come:
Here as before, never, so help you mercy,
170 How strange or odd some'er I bear myself
(As I perchance hereafter shall think meet
To put an antic disposition° on),
That you, at such times seeing me, never shall
With arms encumb'red° thus, or this headshake,
175 Or by pronouncing of some doubtful phrase,
As "Well, well, we know," or "We could, an if we
would,"
Or "If we list to speak," or "There be, an if they
might,"
Or such ambiguous giving out, to note
That you know aught of me—this do swear,
180 So grace and mercy at your most need help you.

Ghost. [*Beneath*] Swear.   [*They swear.*]

Hamlet. Rest, rest, perturbèd spirit. So, gentlemen,
With all my love I do commend me° to you,
And what so poor a man as Hamlet is
185 May do t' express his love and friending to you,
God willing, shall not lack. Let us go in together,
And still your fingers on your lips, I pray.
The time is out of joint. O cursèd spite,
That ever I was born to set it right!
190 Nay, come, let's go together.   *Exeunt.*

172 **antic disposition** fantastic behavior 174 **encumb'red** folded
183 **commend me** entrust myself

[ACT 2

Scene 1. *A room.*]

Enter old Polonius, with his man Reynaldo.

Polonius. Give him this money and these notes, Reynaldo.

Reynaldo. I will, my lord.

Polonius. You shall do marvell's° wisely, good Rey-
   naldo,
   Before you visit him, to make inquire
   Of his behavior.

Reynaldo.   My lord, I did intend it.   5

Polonius. Marry, well said, very well said. Look you
   sir,
   Inquire me first what Danskers° are in Paris,
   And how, and who, what means, and where they
      keep,°
   What company, at what expense; and finding
   By this encompassment° and drift of question   10
   That they do know my son, come you more nearer
   Than your particular demands° will touch it.
   Take you as 'twere some distant knowledge of him,
   As thus, "I know his father and his friends,
   And in part him." Do you mark this, Reynaldo?   15

Reynaldo. Ay, very well, my lord.

2.1.3 **marvell's** marvelous(ly)   7 **Danskers** Danes   8 **keep** dwell
10 **encompassment** circling   12 **demands** questions

35

Polonius. "And in part him, but," you may say, "not
    well,
  But if't be he I mean, he's very wild,
  Addicted so and so." And there put on him
20 What forgeries° you please; marry, none so rank
  As may dishonor him—take heed of that—
  But, sir, such wanton, wild, and usual slips
  As are companions noted and most known
  To youth and liberty.

Reynaldo.   As gaming, my lord.

Polonius. Ay, or drinking, fencing, swearing, quarrel-
25   ing,
  Drabbing.° You may go so far.

Reynaldo. My lord, that would dishonor him.

Polonius. Faith, no, as you may season it in the charge.
  You must not put another scandal on him,
30 That he is open to incontinency.°
  That's not my meaning. But breathe his faults so
    quaintly°
  That they may seem the taints of liberty,
  The flash and outbreak of a fiery mind,
  A savageness in unreclaimèd blood,
  Of general assault.°

35 **Reynaldo.**   But, my good lord——

Polonius. Wherefore should you do this?

Reynaldo.   Ay, my lord,
  I would know that.

Polonius.   Marry, sir, here's my drift,
  And I believe it is a fetch of warrant.°
  You laying these slight sullies on my son
40 As 'twere a thing a little soiled i' th' working,
  Mark you,
  Your party in converse, him you would sound,

---

20 **forgeries** inventions 26 **Drabbing** wenching 30 **incontinency** habitual licentiousness 31 **quaintly** ingeniously, delicately 35 **Of general assault** common to all men 38 **fetch of warrant** justifiable device

Having ever seen in the prenominate crimes°
The youth you breathe of guilty, be assured
He closes with you in this consequence:°　　　　　45
"Good sir," or so, or "friend," or "gentleman"—
According to the phrase or the addition°
Of man and country—

Reynaldo.　　　　　　　　Very good, my lord.

Polonius. And then, sir, does 'a° this—'a does—
What was I about to say? By the mass, I was about　　50
to say something! Where did I leave?

Reynaldo. At "closes in the consequence," at "friend
or so," and "gentleman."

Polonius. At "closes in the consequence"—Ay, marry!
He closes thus: "I know the gentleman;　　　　　55
I saw him yesterday, or t'other day,
Or then, or then, with such or such, and, as you say,
There was 'a gaming, there o'ertook in's rouse,
There falling out at tennis"; or perchance,
"I saw him enter such a house of sale,"　　　　　60
Videlicet,° a brothel, or so forth.
See you now—
Your bait of falsehood take this carp of truth,
And thus do we of wisdom and of reach,°
With windlasses° and with assays of bias,°　　　　65
By indirections find directions out.
So, by my former lecture and advice,
Shall you my son. You have me, have you not?

Reynaldo. My lord, I have.

Polonius.　　　　　　　　God bye ye, fare ye well.

Reynaldo. Good my lord.　　　　　　　　　　70

Polonius. Observe his inclination in yourself.°

---

43 **Having ... crimes** if he has ever seen in the aforementioned crimes
45 **He closes ... this consequence** he falls in with you in this conclusion
47 **addition** title　49 **'a** he　61 **Videlicet** namely　64 **reach** far-reaching awareness (?)　65 **windlasses** circuitous courses　65 **assays of bias** indirect attempts (metaphor from bowling; **bias** = curved course)
71 **in yourself** for yourself

Reynaldo. I shall, my lord.

Polonius. And let him ply his music.

Reynaldo.　　　　　　　　　　　　　　Well, my lord.

Polonius. Farewell.　　　　　　　　　　　*Exit Reynaldo.*

　　　　　　　　Enter Ophelia.

　　　　　　　　How now, Ophelia, what's the matter?

75　*Ophelia.* O my lord, my lord, I have been so affrighted!

Polonius. With what, i' th' name of God?

Ophelia. My lord, as I was sewing in my closet,°
　　　Lord Hamlet, with his doublet all unbraced,°
　　　No hat upon his head, his stockings fouled,
80　　Ungartered, and down-gyvèd° to his ankle,
　　　Pale as his shirt, his knees knocking each other,
　　　And with a look so piteous in purport,°
　　　As if he had been loosèd out of hell
　　　To speak of horrors—he comes before me.

Polonius. Mad for thy love?

85　*Ophelia.*　　　　　　　　　My lord, I do not know,
　　　But truly I do fear it.

Polonius.　　　　　　What said he?

Ophelia. He took me by the wrist and held me hard;
　　　Then goes he to the length of all his arm,
　　　And with his other hand thus o'er his brow
90　　He falls to such perusal of my face
　　　As 'a would draw it. Long stayed he so.
　　　At last, a little shaking of mine arm,
　　　And thrice his head thus waving up and down,
　　　He raised a sigh so piteous and profound
95　　As it did seem to shatter all his bulk
　　　And end his being. That done, he lets me go,
　　　And, with his head over his shoulder turned,
　　　He seemed to find his way without his eyes;

77 **closet** private room　78 **doublet all unbraced** jacket entirely un-
laced　80 **down-gyvèd** hanging down like fetters　82 **purport** expres-
sion

For out o' doors he went without their helps,
And to the last bended their light on me. *100*

Polonius. Come, go with me. I will go seek the King.
This is the very ecstasy° of love,
Whose violent property fordoes° itself
And leads the will to desperate undertakings
As oft as any passions under heaven *105*
That does afflict our natures. I am sorry.
What, have you given him any hard words of late?

Ophelia. No, my good lord; but as you did command,
I did repel his letters and denied
His access to me.

Polonius.   That hath made him mad. *110*
I am sorry that with better heed and judgment
I had not quoted° him. I feared he did but trifle
And meant to wrack thee; but beshrew my jealousy.°
By heaven, it is as proper° to our age
To cast beyond ourselves° in our opinions *115*
As it is common for the younger sort
To lack discretion. Come, go we to the King.
This must be known, which, being kept close, might
   move
More grief to hide than hate to utter love.°
Come.   *Exeunt.* *120*

102 **ecstasy** madness   103 **property fordoes** quality destroys 112 **quoted** noted   113 **beshrew my jealousy** curse on my suspicions   114 **proper** natural   115 **To cast beyond ourselves** to be overcalculating 117–19 **Come, go ... utter love** (the general meaning is that while telling the King of Hamlet's love may anger the King, more grief would come from keeping it secret)

[Scene 2. *The castle.*]

Flourish. Enter King and Queen, Rosencrantz, and
Guildenstern [with others].

King. Welcome, dear Rosencrantz and Guildenstern.
  Moreover that° we much did long to see you,
  The need we have to use you did provoke
  Our hasty sending. Something have you heard
5 Of Hamlet's transformation: so call it,
  Sith° nor th' exterior nor the inward man
  Resembles that it was. What it should be,
  More than his father's death, that thus hath put him
  So much from th' understanding of himself,
10 I cannot dream of. I entreat you both
  That, being of so° young days brought up with him,
  And sith so neighbored to his youth and havior,°
  That you vouchsafe your rest° here in our court
  Some little time, so by your companies
15 To draw him on to pleasures, and to gather
  So much as from occasion you may glean,
  Whether aught to us unknown afflicts him thus,
  That opened° lies within our remedy.

Queen. Good gentlemen, he hath much talked of you,
20 And sure I am, two men there is not living
  To whom he more adheres. If it will please you
  To show us so much gentry° and good will
  As to expend your time with us awhile
  For the supply and profit of our hope,
25 Your visitation shall receive such thanks
  As fits a king's remembrance.

Rosencrantz.   Both your Majesties

2.2.2 **Moreover that** beside the fact that   6 **Sith** since   11 **of so** from
such   12 **youth and havior** behavior in his youth   13 **vouchsafe your
rest** consent to remain   18 **opened** revealed   22 **gentry** courtesy

Might, by the sovereign power you have of us,
Put your dread pleasures more into command
Than to entreaty.

Guildenstern.   But we both obey,
And here give up ourselves in the full bent°   30
To lay our service freely at your feet,
To be commanded.

King. Thanks, Rosencrantz and gentle Guildenstern.

Queen. Thanks, Guildenstern and gentle Rosencrantz.
And I beseech you instantly to visit   35
My too much changèd son. Go, some of you,
And bring these gentlemen where Hamlet is.

Guildenstern. Heavens make our presence and our
     practices
Pleasant and helpful to him!

Queen.   Ay, amen!
     Exeunt Rosencrantz and Guildenstern [*with some
                              Attendants*].

                Enter Polonius.

Polonius. Th' ambassadors from Norway, my good
     lord,   40
Are joyfully returned.

King. Thou still° hast been the father of good news.

Polonius. Have I, my lord? Assure you, my good liege,
I hold my duty, as I hold my soul,
Both to my God and to my gracious king;   45
And I do think, or else this brain of mine
Hunts not the trail of policy so sure°
As it hath used to do, that I have found
The very cause of Hamlet's lunacy.

King. O, speak of that! That do I long to hear.   50

Polonius. Give first admittance to th' ambassadors.
My news shall be the fruit to that great feast.

---

30 **in the full bent** entirely (the figure is of a bow bent to its capacity)   42 **still** always   47 **Hunts not ... so sure** does not follow clues of political doings with such sureness

King. Thyself do grace to them and bring them in.
                                [Exit Polonius.]
He tells me, my dear Gertrude, he hath found
55   The head and source of all your son's distemper.

Queen. I doubt° it is no other but the main,°
His father's death and our o'erhasty marriage.

King. Well, we shall sift him.

     Enter Polonius, Voltemand, and Cornelius.

                    Welcome, my good friends.
Say, Voltemand, what from our brother Norway?

60 *Voltemand.* Most fair return of greetings and desires.
Upon our first,° he sent out to suppress
His nephew's levies, which to him appeared
To be a preparation 'gainst the Polack;
But better looked into, he truly found
65   It was against your Highness, whereat grieved,
That so his sickness, age, and impotence
Was falsely borne in hand,° sends out arrests
On Fortinbras; which he, in brief, obeys,
Receives rebuke from Norway, and in fine,°
70   Makes vow before his uncle never more
To give th' assay° of arms against your Majesty.
Whereon old Norway, overcome with joy,
Gives him threescore thousand crowns in annual fee
And his commission to employ those soldiers,
75   So levied as before, against the Polack,
With an entreaty, herein further shown,
                          [Gives a paper.]
That it might please you to give quiet pass
Through your dominions for this enterprise,
On such regards of safety and allowance°
As therein are set down.

80 *King.*   It likes us well;
And at our more considered time° we'll read,
Answer, and think upon this business.

56 doubt suspect **56 main** principal point **61 first** first audience
67 borne in hand deceived **69 in fine** finally **71 assay** trial **79 regards of safety and allowance** i.e., conditions **81 considered time**
time proper for considering

Meantime, we thank you for your well-took labor.
Go to your rest; at night we'll feast together.
Most welcome home!   *Exeunt Ambassadors.*

Polonius.   This business is well ended.   *85*
My liege and madam, to expostulate°
What majesty should be, what duty is,
Why day is day, night night, and time is time,
Were nothing but to waste night, day, and time.
Therefore, since brevity is the soul of wit,°   *90*
And tediousness the limbs and outward flourishes,
I will be brief. Your noble son is mad.
Mad call I it, for, to define true madness,
What is't but to be nothing else but mad?
But let that go.

Queen.   More matter, with less art.   *95*

Polonius. Madam, I swear I use no art at all.
That he's mad, 'tis true: 'tis true 'tis pity,
And pity 'tis 'tis true—a foolish figure.°
But farewell it, for I will use no art.
Mad let us grant him then; and now remains   *100*
That we find out the cause of this effect,
Or rather say, the cause of this defect,
For this effect defective comes by cause.
Thus it remains, and the remainder thus.
Perpend.°   *105*
I have a daughter: have, while she is mine,
Who in her duty and obedience, mark,
Hath given me this. Now gather, and surmise.
                        [*Reads*] *the letter.*
"To the celestial, and my soul's idol, the most
beautified Ophelia"—   *110*
That's an ill phrase, a vile phrase; "beautified" is a
vile phrase. But you shall hear. Thus:
"In her excellent white bosom, these, &c."

Queen. Came this from Hamlet to her?

Polonius. Good madam, stay awhile. I will be faithful.   *115*
            "Doubt thou the stars are fire,

86 **expostulate** discuss   90 **wit** wisdom, understanding   98 **figure** figure of rhetoric   105 **Perpend** consider carefully

> Doubt that the sun doth move;
> Doubt° truth to be a liar,
> But never doubt I love.

120   O dear Ophelia, I am ill at these numbers.° I have
not art to reckon my groans; but that I love thee
best, O most best, believe it. Adieu.

> Thine evermore, most dear lady, whilst this
> machine° is to him, HAMLET."

125   This in obedience hath my daughter shown me,
And more above° hath his solicitings,
As they fell out by time, by means, and place,
All given to mine ear.

King.   But how hath she
Received his love?

Polonius.   What do you think of me?

130   *King.* As of a man faithful and honorable.

Polonius. I would fain prove so. But what might you
think,
When I had seen this hot love on the wing
(As I perceived it, I must tell you that,
Before my daughter told me), what might you,
135   Or my dear Majesty your Queen here, think,
If I had played the desk or table book,°
Or given my heart a winking,° mute and dumb,
Or looked upon this love with idle sight?
What might you think? No, I went round to work
140   And my young mistress thus I did bespeak:
"Lord Hamlet is a prince, out of thy star.°
This must not be." And then I prescripts gave her,
That she should lock herself from his resort,
Admit no messengers, receive no tokens.
145   Which done, she took the fruits of my advice,
And he, repellèd, a short tale to make,

118 **Doubt** suspect   120 **ill at these numbers** unskilled in verses
124 **machine** complex device (here, his body)   126 **more above** in addition   136 **played the desk or table book** i.e., been a passive recipient of
secrets   137 **winking** closing of the eyes   141 **star** sphere

Fell into a sadness, then into a fast,
Thence to a watch,° thence into a weakness,
Thence to a lightness,° and, by this declension,
Into the madness wherein now he raves,   150
And all we mourn for.

King.   Do you think 'tis this?

Queen. It may be, very like.

Polonius. Hath there been such a time, I would fain
     know that,
     That I have positively said " 'Tis so,"
     When it proved otherwise?

King.   Not that I know.   155

Polonius. [*Pointing to his head and shoulder*] Take
     this from this, if this be otherwise.
     If circumstances lead me, I will find
     Where truth is hid, though it were hid indeed
     Within the center.°

King.   How may we try it further?

Polonius. You know sometimes he walks four hours
     together   160
     Here in the lobby.

Queen.   So he does indeed.

Polonius. At such a time I'll loose my daughter to him.
     Be you and I behind an arras° then.
     Mark the encounter. If he love her not,
     And be not from his reason fall'n thereon,   165
     Let me be no assistant for a state
     But keep a farm and carters.

King.   We will try it.

                    Enter Hamlet reading on a book.

Queen. But look where sadly the poor wretch comes
     reading.

Polonius. Away, I do beseech you both, away.

                                   Exit King and Queen.

---

148 **watch** wakefulness   149 **lightness** mental derangement   159 **cen-**
ter center of the earth   163 **arras** tapestry hanging in front of a wall

170   I'll board him presently.° O, give me leave.
How does my good Lord Hamlet?

Hamlet. Well, God-a-mercy.

Polonius. Do you know me, my lord?

Hamlet. Excellent well. You are a fishmonger.°

175 *Polonius.* Not I, my lord.

Hamlet. Then I would you were so honest a man.

Polonius. Honest, my lord?

Hamlet. Ay, sir. To be honest, as this world goes, is to
be one man picked out of ten thousand.

180 *Polonius.* That's very true, my lord.

Hamlet. For if the sun breed maggots in a dead dog,
being a good kissing carrion°—— Have you a
daughter?

Polonius. I have, my lord.

185 *Hamlet.* Let her not walk i' th' sun. Conception° is a
blessing, but as your daughter may conceive, friend,
look to 't.

Polonius. [*Aside*] How say you by that? Still harping
on my daughter. Yet he knew me not at first. 'A said
190 I was a fishmonger. 'A is far gone, far gone. And
truly in my youth I suffered much extremity for
love, very near this. I'll speak to him again.—What
do you read, my lord?

Hamlet. Words, words, words.

195 *Polonius.* What is the matter, my lord?

Hamlet. Between who?

Polonius. I mean the matter° that you read, my lord.

***

170 **board him presently** accost him at once   174 **fishmonger** dealer
in fish (slang for a procurer). (The joke is in the inappropriateness. Al-
though many editors say that *fishmonger* is slang for a procurer, such us-
age is undocumented)   182 **a good kissing carrion** (perhaps the
meaning is "a good piece of flesh to kiss," but many editors emend *good*
to *god,* taking the word to refer to the sun)   185 **Conception** (1) understanding (2) becoming pregnant   197 **matter** (Polonius means "subject
matter," but Hamlet pretends to take the word in the sense of "quarrel")

Hamlet. Slanders, sir; for the satirical rogue says here
   that old men have gray beards, that their faces are
   wrinkled, their eyes purging thick amber and plum-   *200*
   tree gum, and that they have a plentiful lack of wit,
   together with most weak hams. All which, sir,
   though I most powerfully and potently believe, yet
   I hold it not honesty° to have it thus set down; for
   you yourself, sir, should be old as I am if, like a   *205*
   crab, you could go backward.

Polonius. [*Aside*] Though this be madness, yet there
   is method in't. Will you walk out of the air, my lord?

Hamlet. Into my grave.

Polonius. Indeed, that's out of the air. [*Aside*] How   *210*
   pregnant° sometimes his replies are! A happiness°
   that often madness hits on, which reason and sanity
   could not so prosperously be delivered of. I will
   leave him and suddenly contrive the means of
   meeting between him and my daughter.—My lord,   *215*
   I will take my leave of you.

Hamlet. You cannot take from me anything that I will
   more willingly part withal—except my life, except
   my life, except my life.

           Enter Guildenstern and Rosencrantz.

Polonius. Fare you well, my lord.   *220*

Hamlet. These tedious old fools!

Polonius. You go to seek the Lord Hamlet? There he
   is.

Rosencrantz. [*To Polonius*] God save you, sir!
                                  [*Exit Polonius.*]

Guildenstern. My honored lord!   *225*

Rosencrantz. My most dear lord!

Hamlet. My excellent good friends! How dost thou,
   Guildenstern? Ah, Rosencrantz! Good lads, how do
   you both?

204 **honesty** decency   211 **pregnant** meaningful   211 **happiness** apt
turn of phrase

230 *Rosencrantz.* As the indifferent° children of the earth.

Guildenstern. Happy in that we are not overhappy.
 On Fortune's cap we are not the very button.

Hamlet. Nor the soles of her shoe?

Rosencrantz. Neither, my lord.

235 *Hamlet.* Then you live about her waist, or in the middle
 of her favors?

Guildenstern. Faith, her privates° we.

Hamlet. In the secret parts of Fortune? O, most true!
 She is a strumpet. What news?

240 *Rosencrantz.* None, my lord, but that the world's
 grown honest.

Hamlet. Then is doomsday near. But your news is not
 true. Let me question more in particular. What
 have you, my good friends, deserved at the hands of
245 Fortune that she sends you to prison hither?

Guildenstern. Prison, my lord?

Hamlet. Denmark's a prison.

Rosencrantz. Then is the world one.

Hamlet. A goodly one, in which there are many
250 confines, wards,° and dungeons, Denmark being
 one o' th' worst.

Rosencrantz. We think not so, my lord.

Hamlet. Why, then 'tis none to you, for there is nothing
 either good or bad but thinking makes it so. To me
255 it is a prison.

Rosencrantz. Why then your ambition makes it one.
 'Tis too narrow for your mind.

Hamlet. O God, I could be bounded in a nutshell and
 count myself a king of infinite space, were it not
260 that I have bad dreams.

Guildenstern. Which dreams indeed are ambition, for

---

230 **indifferent** ordinary   237 **privates** ordinary men (with a pun on
"private parts")   250 **wards** cells

the very substance of the ambitious is merely the
shadow of a dream.

Hamlet. A dream itself is but a shadow.

Rosencrantz. Truly, and I hold ambition of so airy and   265
light a quality that it is but a shadow's shadow.

Hamlet. Then are our beggars bodies, and our
monarchs and outstretched heroes the beggars'
shadows.° Shall we to th' court? For, by my fay,°
I cannot reason.   270

Both. We'll wait upon you.

Hamlet. No such matter. I will not sort you with the
rest of my servants, for, to speak to you like an
honest man, I am most dreadfully attended. But in
the beaten way of friendship, what make you at   275
Elsinore?

Rosencrantz. To visit you, my lord; no other occasion.

Hamlet. Beggar that I am, I am even poor in thanks,
but I thank you; and sure, dear friends, my thanks
are too dear a halfpenny.° Were you not sent for?   280
Is it your own inclining? Is it a free visitation?
Come, come, deal justly with me. Come, come;
nay, speak.

Guildenstern. What should we say, my lord?

Hamlet. Why anything—but to th' purpose. You were   285
sent for, and there is a kind of confession in your
looks, which your modesties have not craft enough
to color. I know the good King and Queen have
sent for you.

Rosencrantz. To what end, my lord?   290

Hamlet. That you must teach me. But let me conjure
you by the rights of our fellowship, by the con-
sonancy of our youth, by the obligation of our ever-

267–69 **Then are ... beggars' shadows** i.e., by your logic, beggars
(lacking ambition) are substantial, and great men are elongated shadows
269 **fay** faith   280 **too dear a halfpenny** i.e., not worth a halfpenny

295 preserved love, and by what more dear a better proposer can charge you withal, be even and direct with me, whether you were sent for or no.

Rosencrantz. [*Aside to Guildenstern*] What say you?

Hamlet. [*Aside*] Nay then, I have an eye of you.—If you love me, hold not off.

300 *Guildenstern.* My lord, we were sent for.

Hamlet. I will tell you why; so shall my anticipation prevent your discovery,° and your secrecy to the King and Queen molt no feather. I have of late, but wherefore I know not, lost all my mirth, forgone all
305 custom of exercises; and indeed, it goes so heavily with my disposition that this goodly frame, the earth, seems to me a sterile promontory; this most excellent canopy, the air, look you, this brave o'erhanging firmament, this majestical roof fretted°
310 with golden fire: why, it appeareth nothing to me but a foul and pestilent congregation of vapors. What a piece of work is a man, how noble in reason, how infinite in faculties, in form and moving how express° and admirable, in action how like an angel,
315 in apprehension how like a god: the beauty of the world, the paragon of animals; and yet to me, what is this quintessence of dust? Man delights not me; nor woman neither, though by your smiling you seem to say so.

320 *Rosencrantz.* My lord, there was no such stuff in my thoughts.

Hamlet. Why did ye laugh then, when I said "Man delights not me"?

Rosencrantz. To think, my lord, if you delight not in
325 man, what lenten° entertainment the players shall receive from you. We coted° them on the way, and hither are they coming to offer you service.

---

302 **prevent your discovery** forestall your disclosure   309 **fretted** adorned   314 **express** exact   325 **lenten** meager   326 **coted** overtook

Hamlet. He that plays the king shall be welcome; his
Majesty shall have tribute of me; the adventurous
knight shall use his foil and target;° the lover shall   330
not sigh gratis; the humorous man° shall end his
part in peace; the clown shall make those laugh
whose lungs are tickle o' th' sere;° and the lady shall
say her mind freely, or° the blank verse shall halt°
for't. What players are they?   335

Rosencrantz. Even those you were wont to take such
delight in, the tragedians of the city.

Hamlet. How chances it they travel? Their residence,
both in reputation and profit, was better both ways.

Rosencrantz. I think their inhibition° comes by the   340
means of the late innovation.°

Hamlet. Do they hold the same estimation they did
when I was in the city? Are they so followed?

Rosencrantz. No indeed, are they not.

Hamlet. How comes it? Do they grow rusty?   345

Rosencrantz. Nay, their endeavor keeps in the wonted
pace, but there is, sir, an eyrie° of children, little
eyases, that cry out on the top of question° and are
most tyrannically° clapped for't. These are now
the fashion, and so berattle the common stages° (so   350
they call them) that many wearing rapiers are afraid
of goosequills° and dare scarce come thither.

Hamlet. What, are they children? Who maintains 'em?
How are they escoted?° Will they pursue the

---

330 **target** shield   331 **humorous man** i.e., eccentric man (among
stock characters in dramas were men dominated by a "humor" or odd
trait)   333 **tickle o' th' sere** on hair trigger (*sere* = part of the gunlock)
334 **or** else   334 **halt** limp   340 **inhibition** hindrance   341 **innovation** (probably an allusion to the companies of child actors that had become popular and were offering serious competition to the adult actors)
347 **eyrie** nest   348 **eyases, that . . . of question** unfledged hawks that
cry shrilly above others in matters of debate   349 **tyrannically** vio-
lently   350 **berattle the common stages** cry down the public theaters
(with the adult acting companies)   352 **goosequills** pens (of satirists
who ridicule the public theaters and their audiences)   354 **escoted** fi-
nancially supported

355 quality° no longer than they can sing? Will they not
say afterwards, if they should grow themselves to
common players (as it is most like, if their means
are no better), their writers do them wrong to make
them exclaim against their own succession?°

360 *Rosencrantz.* Faith, there has been much to-do on
both sides, and the nation holds it no sin to tarre°
them to controversy. There was, for a while, no
money bid for argument° unless the poet and the
player went to cuffs in the question.

365 *Hamlet.* Is't possible?

Guildenstern. O, there has been much throwing about
of brains.

Hamlet. Do the boys carry it away?

Rosencrantz. Ay, that they do, my lord—Hercules and
370 his load° too.

Hamlet. It is not very strange, for my uncle is King of
Denmark, and those that would make mouths at
him while my father lived give twenty, forty, fifty,
a hundred ducats apiece for his picture in little.
375 'Sblood,° there is something in this more than
natural, if philosophy could find it out.

A flourish.

Guildenstern. There are the players.

Hamlet. Gentlemen, you are welcome to Elsinore.
Your hands, come then. Th' appurtenance of wel-
380 come is fashion and ceremony. Let me comply°
with you in this garb,° lest my extent° to the players
(which I tell you must show fairly outwards) should
more appear like entertainment than yours. You are
welcome. But my uncle-father and aunt-mother are
385 deceived.

355 **quality** profession of acting   359 **succession** future   361 **tarre** incite   363 **argument** plot of a play   369–70 **Hercules and his load** i.e.,
the whole world (with a reference to the Globe Theatre, which had a
sign that represented Hercules bearing the globe)   375 **'Sblood** by
God's blood   380 **comply** be courteous   381 **garb** outward show
381 **extent** behavior

Guildenstern. In what, my dear lord?

Hamlet. I am but mad north-northwest:° when the
wind is southerly I know a hawk from a handsaw.°

Enter Polonius.

Polonius. Well be with you, gentlemen.

Hamlet. Hark you, Guildenstern, and you too; at each   *390*
ear a hearer. That great baby you see there is not
yet out of his swaddling clouts.

Rosencrantz. Happily° he is the second time come to
them, for they say an old man is twice a child.

Hamlet. I will prophesy he comes to tell me of the   *395*
players. Mark it.—You say right, sir; a Monday
morning, 'twas then indeed.

Polonius. My lord, I have news to tell you.

Hamlet. My lord, I have news to tell you. When
Roscius° was an actor in Rome——   *400*

Polonius. The actors are come hither, my lord.

Hamlet. Buzz, buzz.°

Polonius. Upon my honor——

Hamlet. Then came each actor on his ass——

Polonius. The best actors in the world, either for   *405*
tragedy, comedy, history, pastoral, pastoral-comical,
historical-pastoral, tragical-historical, tragical-comi-
cal-historical-pastoral; scene individable,° or poem
unlimited.° Seneca° cannot be too heavy, nor
Plautus° too light. For the law of writ and the   *410*
liberty,° these are the only men.

---

387 **north-northwest** i.e., on one point of the compass only   388 **hawk
from a handsaw** (**hawk** can refer not only to a bird but to a kind of
pickax; **handsaw**—a carpenter's tool—may involve a similar pun on
"hernshaw," a heron)   393 **Happily** perhaps   400 **Roscius** (a famous
Roman comic actor)   402 **Buzz, buzz** (an interjection, perhaps indicat-
ing that the news is old)   408 **scene individable** plays observing the
unities of time, place, and action   408–09 **poem unlimited** plays not
restricted by the tenets of criticism   409 **Seneca** (Roman tragic dramatist)   410 **Plautus** (Roman comic dramatist)   410–11 **For the law of
writ and the liberty** (perhaps "for sticking to the text and for improvis-
ing"; perhaps "for classical plays and for modern loosely written plays")

Hamlet. O Jeptha, judge of Israel,° what a treasure
hadst thou!

Polonius. What a treasure had he, my lord?

415 *Hamlet.* Why,
   "One fair daughter, and no more,
    The which he lovèd passing well."

Polonius. [*Aside*] Still on my daughter.

Hamlet. Am I not i' th' right, old Jeptha?

420 *Polonius.* If you call me Jeptha, my lord, I have a
daughter that I love passing well.

Hamlet. Nay, that follows not.

Polonius. What follows then, my lord?

Hamlet. Why,

425   "As by lot, God wot,"
and then, you know,
   "It came to pass, as most like it was."
The first row of the pious chanson° will show you
more, for look where my abridgment° comes.

Enter the Players.

430 You are welcome, masters, welcome, all. I am glad
to see thee well. Welcome, good friends. O, old
friend, why, thy face is valanced° since I saw thee
last. Com'st thou to beard me in Denmark? What,
my young lady° and mistress? By'r Lady, your

435 ladyship is nearer to heaven than when I saw you
last by the altitude of a chopine.° Pray God your
voice, like a piece of uncurrent gold, be not cracked
within the ring.°—Masters, you are all welcome.
We'll e'en to 't like French falconers, fly at any-

---

412 **Jeptha, judge of Israel** (the title of a ballad on the Hebrew judge
who sacrificed his daughter; see Judges 11) 428 **row of the pious
chanson** stanza of the scriptural song 429 **abridgment** (1) i.e., enter-
tainers, who abridge the time (2) interrupters 432 **valanced** fringed
(with a beard) 434 **young lady** i.e., boy for female roles 436 **chopine**
thick-soled shoe 437–38 **like a piece ... the ring** (a coin was unfit for
legal tender if a crack extended from the edge through the ring enclosing
the monarch's head. Hamlet, punning on *ring*, refers to the change of
voice that the boy actor will undergo)

thing we see. We'll have a speech straight. Come, 440
give us a taste of your quality. Come, a passionate
speech.

Player. What speech, my good lord?

Hamlet. I heard thee speak me a speech once, but it
was never acted, or if it was, not above once, for 445
the play, I remember, pleased not the million; 'twas
caviary to the general,° but it was (as I received it,
and others, whose judgments in such matters cried
in the top of° mine) an excellent play, well digested
in the scenes, set down with as much modesty as 450
cunning.° I remember one said there were no
sallets° in the lines to make the matter savory;
nor no matter in the phrase that might indict the
author of affectation, but called it an honest method,
as wholesome as sweet, and by very much more 455
handsome than fine.° One speech in't I chiefly loved.
'Twas Aeneas' tale to Dido, and thereabout of it
especially when he speaks of Priam's slaughter. If
it live in your memory, begin at this line—let me
see, let me see: 460
  "The rugged Pyrrhus, like th' Hyrcanian
      beast°——"
'Tis not so; it begins with Pyrrhus:
  "The rugged Pyrrhus, he whose sable° arms,
  Black as his purpose, did the night resemble
  When he lay couchèd in th' ominous horse,° 465
  Hath now this dread and black complexion
      smeared
  With heraldry more dismal.° Head to foot
  Now is he total gules, horridly tricked°
  With blood of fathers, mothers, daughters, sons,
  Baked and impasted° with the parching streets, 470

447 **caviary to the general** i.e., too choice for the multitude 449 **in the top of** overtopping 450–51 **modesty as cunning** restraint as art 452 **sallets** salads, spicy jests 455–56 **more handsome than fine** well-proportioned rather than ornamented 461 **Hyrcanian beast** i.e., tiger (Hyrcania was in Asia) 463 **sable** black 465 **ominous horse** i.e., wooden horse at the siege of Troy 467 **dismal** ill-omened 468 **total gules, horridly tricked** all red, horridly adorned 470 **impasted** encrusted

That lend a tyrannous and a damnèd light
To their lord's murder. Roasted in wrath and fire,
And thus o'ersizèd° with coagulate gore,
With eyes like carbuncles, the hellish Pyrrhus
475 Old grandsire Priam seeks."
So, proceed you.

Polonius. Fore God, my lord, well spoken, with good
accent and good discretion.

Player.   "Anon he finds him,
480 Striking too short at Greeks. His antique sword,
Rebellious to his arm, lies where it falls,
Repugnant to command.° Unequal matched,
Pyrrhus at Priam drives, in rage strikes wide,
But with the whiff and wind of his fell sword
485 Th' unnervèd father falls. Then senseless Ilium,°
Seeming to feel this blow, with flaming top
Stoops to his base,° and with a hideous crash
Takes prisoner Pyrrhus' ear. For lo, his sword,
Which was declining on the milky head
490 Of reverend Priam, seemed i' th' air to stick.
So as a painted tyrant° Pyrrhus stood,
And like a neutral to his will and matter°
Did nothing.
But as we often see, against° some storm,
495 A silence in the heavens, the rack° stand still,
The bold winds speechless, and the orb below
As hush as death, anon the dreadful thunder
Doth rend the region, so after Pyrrhus' pause,
A rousèd vengeance sets him new awork,
500 And never did the Cyclops' hammer fall
On Mars's armor, forged for proof eterne,°
With less remorse than Pyrrhus' bleeding sword
Now falls on Priam.
Out, out, thou strumpet Fortune! All you gods,
505 In general synod° take away her power,

473 **o'ersizèd** smeared over   482 **Repugnant to command** disobedient
485 **senseless Ilium** insensate Troy   487 **Stoops to his base** collapses
(*his* = its)   491 **painted tyrant** tyrant in a picture   492 **matter** task
494 **against** just before   495 **rack** clouds   501 **proof eterne** eternal
endurance   505 **synod** council

Break all the spokes and fellies° from her wheel,
And bowl the round nave° down the hill of
　heaven,
As low as to the fiends."

Polonius. This is too long.

Hamlet. It shall to the barber's, with your beard.— 510
　Prithee say on. He's for a jig or a tale of bawdry,
　or he sleeps. Say on; come to Hecuba.

Player. "But who (ah woe!) had seen the mobled°
　queen——"

Hamlet. "The mobled queen"?

Polonius. That's good. "Mobled queen" is good. 515

Player. "Run barefoot up and down, threat'ning the
　flames
With bisson rheum;° a clout° upon that head
Where late the diadem stood, and for a robe,
About her lank and all o'erteemèd° loins,
A blanket in the alarm of fear caught up— 520
Who this had seen, with tongue in venom steeped
'Gainst Fortune's state would treason have pro-
　nounced.
But if the gods themselves did see her then,
When she saw Pyrrhus make malicious sport
In mincing with his sword her husband's limbs, 525
The instant burst of clamor that she made
(Unless things mortal move them not at all)
Would have made milch° the burning eyes of
　heaven
And passion in the gods."

Polonius. Look, whe'r° he has not turned his color, 530
　and has tears in's eyes. Prithee no more.

Hamlet. 'Tis well. I'll have thee speak out the rest of
　this soon. Good my lord, will you see the players
　well bestowed?° Do you hear? Let them be well

506 **fellies** rims　507 **nave** hub　513 **mobled** muffled　517 **bisson rheum** blinding tears　517 **clout** rag　519 **o'erteemèd** exhausted with childbearing　528 **milch** moist (literally, "milk-giving")　530 **whe'r** whether　534 **bestowed** housed

535   used, for they are the abstract and brief chronicles
of the time. After your death you were better have
a bad epitaph than their ill report while you live.

Polonius. My lord, I will use them according to their
desert.

540   *Hamlet.* God's bodkin,° man, much better! Use every
man after his desert, and who shall scape whipping?
Use them after your own honor and dignity. The
less they deserve, the more merit is in your bounty.
Take them in.

545   *Polonius.* Come, sirs.

Hamlet. Follow him, friends. We'll hear a play tomorrow. [*Aside to Player*] Dost thou hear me, old
friend? Can you play *The Murder of Gonzago*?

Player. Ay, my lord.

550   *Hamlet.* We'll ha't tomorrow night. You could for a
need study a speech of some dozen or sixteen lines
which I would set down and insert in't, could you
not?

Player. Ay, my lord.

555   *Hamlet.* Very well. Follow that lord, and look you
mock him not. My good friends, I'll leave you till
night. You are welcome to Elsinore.
                                   Exeunt Polonius and Players.

Rosencrantz. Good my lord.
                        Exeunt [Rosencrantz and Guildenstern].

Hamlet. Ay, so, God bye to you.—Now I am alone.
560   O, what a rogue and peasant slave am I!
Is it not monstrous that this player here,
But in a fiction, in a dream of passion,°
Could force his soul so to his own conceit°
That from her working all his visage wanned,
565   Tears in his eyes, distraction in his aspect,
A broken voice, and his whole function° suiting

540 **God's bodkin** by God's little body   562 **dream of passion** imagi-
nary emotion   563 **conceit** imagination   566 **function** action

With forms° to his conceit? And all for nothing!
For Hecuba!
What's Hecuba to him, or he to Hecuba,
That he should weep for her? What would he do   *570*
Had he the motive and the cue for passion
That I have? He would drown the stage with tears
And cleave the general ear with horrid speech,
Make mad the guilty and appall the free,°
Confound the ignorant, and amaze indeed   *575*
The very faculties of eyes and ears.
Yet I,
A dull and muddy-mettled° rascal, peak
Like John-a-dreams,° unpregnant of° my cause,
And can say nothing. No, not for a king,   *580*
Upon whose property and most dear life
A damned defeat was made. Am I a coward?
Who calls me villain? Breaks my pate across?
Plucks off my beard and blows it in my face?
Tweaks me by the nose? Gives me the lie i' th' throat *585*
As deep as to the lungs? Who does me this?
Ha, 'swounds,° I should take it, for it cannot be
But I am pigeon-livered° and lack gall
To make oppression bitter, or ere this
I should ha' fatted all the region kites°   *590*
With this slave's offal. Bloody, bawdy villain!
Remorseless, treacherous, lecherous, kindless° vil-
    lain!
O, vengeance!
Why, what an ass am I! This is most brave,°
That I, the son of a dear father murdered,   *595*
Prompted to my revenge by heaven and hell,
Must, like a whore, unpack my heart with words
And fall a-cursing like a very drab,°

---

567 **forms** bodily expressions   574 **appall the free** terrify (make pale?)
the guiltless   578 **muddy-mettled** weak-spirited   578–79 **peak/Like
John-a-dreams** mope like a dreamer   579 **unpregnant of** unquickened
by   587 **'swounds** by God's wounds   588 **pigeon-livered** gentle as a
dove   590 **region kites** kites (scavenger birds) of the sky   592 **kind-
less** unnatural   594 **brave** fine   598 **drab** prostitute

A scullion!° Fie upon't, foh! About,° my brains.
600   Hum——
      I have heard that guilty creatures sitting at a play
      Have by the very cunning of the scene
      Been struck so to the soul that presently°
      They have proclaimed their malefactions.
605   For murder, though it have no tongue, will speak
      With most miraculous organ. I'll have these players
      Play something like the murder of my father
      Before mine uncle. I'll observe his looks,
      I'll tent° him to the quick. If 'a do blench,°
610   I know my course. The spirit that I have seen
      May be a devil, and the devil hath power
      T' assume a pleasing shape, yea, and perhaps
      Out of my weakness and my melancholy,
      As he is very potent with such spirits,
615   Abuses me to damn me. I'll have grounds
      More relative° than this. The play's the thing
      Wherein I'll catch the conscience of the King.   *Exit.*

599 **scullion** low-ranking kitchen servant, noted for foul language
599 **About** to work   603 **presently** immediately   609 **tent** probe
609 **blench** flinch   616 **relative** (probably "pertinent," but possibly
"able to be related plausibly")

[ACT 3

Scene 1. *The castle.*]

Enter King, Queen, Polonius, Ophelia, Rosencrantz,
Guildenstern, Lords.

King. And can you by no drift of conference°
    Get from him why he puts on this confusion,
    Grating so harshly all his days of quiet
    With turbulent and dangerous lunacy?

Rosencrantz. He does confess he feels himself dis-
    tracted,   5
    But from what cause 'a will by no means speak.

Guildenstern. Nor do we find him forward to be
    sounded,°
    But with a crafty madness keeps aloof
    When we would bring him on to some confession
    Of his true state.

Queen.   Did he receive you well?   10

Rosencrantz. Most like a gentleman.

Guildenstern. But with much forcing of his disposi-
    tion.°

Rosencrantz. Niggard of question,° but of our demands
    Most free in his reply.

3.1.1 **drift of conference** management of conversation   7 **forward to
be sounded** willing to be questioned   12 **forcing of his disposition** ef-
fort   13 **Niggard of question** uninclined to talk

Queen.   Did you assay° him
15   To any pastime?

Rosencrantz. Madam, it so fell out that certain players
        We o'erraught° on the way; of these we told him,
        And there did seem in him a kind of joy
        To hear of it. They are here about the court,
20   And, as I think, they have already order
        This night to play before him.

Polonius.   'Tis most true,
        And he beseeched me to entreat your Majesties
        To hear and see the matter.

King. With all my heart, and it doth much content me
25   To hear him so inclined.
        Good gentlemen, give him a further edge
        And drive his purpose into these delights.

Rosencrantz. We shall, my lord.
                    Exeunt Rosencrantz and Guildenstern.

King.   Sweet Gertrude, leave us too,
        For we have closely° sent for Hamlet hither,
30   That he, as 'twere by accident, may here
        Affront° Ophelia.
        Her father and myself (lawful espials°)
        Will so bestow ourselves that, seeing unseen,
        We may of their encounter frankly judge
35   And gather by him, as he is behaved,
        If't be th' affliction of his love or no
        That thus he suffers for.

Queen.   I shall obey you.
        And for your part, Ophelia, I do wish
        That your good beauties be the happy cause
40   Of Hamlet's wildness. So shall I hope your virtues
        Will bring him to his wonted way again,
        To both your honors.

Ophelia.   Madam, I wish it may.
                              [*Exit Queen.*]

---

14 **assay** tempt   17 **o'erraught** overtook   29 **closely** secretly   31 **Affront** meet face to face   32 **espials** spies

Polonius. Ophelia, walk you here.—Gracious, so please
    you,
  We will bestow ourselves. [*To Ophelia*] Read on this
    book,
  That show of such an exercise may color°   *45*
  Your loneliness. We are oft to blame in this,
  'Tis too much proved, that with devotion's visage
  And pious action we do sugar o'er
  The devil himself.

King.   [*Aside*] O, 'tis too true.
  How smart a lash that speech doth give my con-
    science!   *50*
  The harlot's cheek, beautied with plast'ring art,
  Is not more ugly to the thing that helps it
  Than is my deed to my most painted word.
  O heavy burden!

Polonius. I hear him coming. Let's withdraw, my lord.   *55*
          [*Exeunt King and Polonius.*]
      Enter Hamlet.

Hamlet. To be, or not to be: that is the question:
  Whether 'tis nobler in the mind to suffer
  The slings and arrows of outrageous fortune,
  Or to take arms against a sea of troubles,
  And by opposing end them. To die, to sleep—   *60*
  No more—and by a sleep to say we end
  The heartache, and the thousand natural shocks
  That flesh is heir to! 'Tis a consummation
  Devoutly to be wished. To die, to sleep—
  To sleep—perchance to dream: ay, there's the rub,°   *65*
  For in that sleep of death what dreams may come
  When we have shuffled off this mortal coil,°
  Must give us pause. There's the respect°
  That makes calamity of so long life:°
  For who would bear the whips and scorns of time,   *70*

45 **exercise may color** act of devotion may give a plausible hue to (the
book is one of devotion)   65 **rub** impediment (obstruction to a bowler's
ball)   67 **coil** (1) turmoil (2) a ring of rope (here the flesh encircling the
soul)   68 **respect** consideration   69 **makes calamity of so long life** (1)
makes calamity so long-lived (2) makes living so long a calamity

Th' oppressor's wrong, the proud man's contumely,
The pangs of despised love, the law's delay,
The insolence of office, and the spurns
That patient merit of th' unworthy takes,
75   When he himself might his quietus° make
With a bare bodkin?° Who would fardels° bear,
To grunt and sweat under a weary life,
But that the dread of something after death,
The undiscovered country, from whose bourn°
80   No traveler returns, puzzles the will,
And makes us rather bear those ills we have,
Than fly to others that we know not of?
Thus conscience° does make cowards of us all,
And thus the native hue of resolution
85   Is sicklied o'er with the pale cast° of thought,
And enterprises of great pitch° and moment,
With this regard° their currents turn awry,
And lose the name of action.—Soft you now,
The fair Ophelia!—Nymph, in thy orisons°
Be all my sins remembered.

90 *Ophelia.*   Good my lord,
How does your honor for this many a day?

Hamlet. I humbly thank you; well, well, well.

Ophelia. My lord, I have remembrances of yours
That I have longèd long to redeliver.
I pray you now, receive them.

95 *Hamlet.*   No, not I,
I never gave you aught.

Ophelia. My honored lord, you know right well you
    did,
And with them words of so sweet breath composed
As made these things more rich. Their perfume lost,
100   Take these again, for to the noble mind

---

75 **quietus** full discharge (a legal term) 76 **bodkin** dagger 76 **fardels**
burdens 79 **bourn** region 83 **conscience** (1) self-consciousness, in-
trospection (2) inner moral voice 85 **cast** color 86 **pitch** height (a
term from falconry) 87 **regard** consideration 89 **orisons** prayers

Rich gifts wax poor when givers prove unkind.
There, my lord.

Hamlet. Ha, ha! Are you honest?°

Ophelia. My lord?

Hamlet. Are you fair? 105

Ophelia. What means your lordship?

Hamlet. That if you be honest and fair, your honesty should admit no discourse to your beauty.°

Ophelia. Could beauty, my lord, have better commerce than with honesty? 110

Hamlet. Ay, truly; for the power of beauty will sooner transform honesty from what it is to a bawd° than the force of honesty can translate beauty into his likeness. This was sometime a paradox, but now the time gives it proof. I did love you once. 115

Ophelia. Indeed, my lord, you made me believe so.

Hamlet. You should not have believed me, for virtue cannot so inoculate° our old stock but we shall relish of it.° I loved you not.

Ophelia. I was the more deceived. 120

Hamlet. Get thee to a nunnery. Why wouldst thou be a breeder of sinners? I am myself indifferent honest,° but yet I could accuse me of such things that it were better my mother had not borne me: I am very proud, revengeful, ambitious, with more offenses at 125 my beck° than I have thoughts to put them in, imagination to give them shape, or time to act them in. What should such fellows as I do crawling between earth and heaven? We are arrant knaves all; believe none of us. Go thy ways to a nunnery. 130 Where's your father?

103 **Are you honest** (1) are you modest (2) are you chaste (3) have you integrity　107–08 **your honesty ... to your beauty** your modesty should permit no approach to your beauty　112 **bawd** procurer 118 **inoculate** graft　118–19 **relish of it** smack of it (our old sinful nature)　122 **indifferent honest** moderately virtuous　126 **beck** call

Ophelia. At home, my lord.

Hamlet. Let the doors be shut upon him, that he may play the fool nowhere but in's own house. Farewell.

135　*Ophelia.* O help him, you sweet heavens!

Hamlet. If thou dost marry, I'll give thee this plague for thy dowry: be thou as chaste as ice, as pure as snow, thou shalt not escape calumny. Get thee to a nunnery. Go, farewell. Or if thou wilt needs marry,
140　marry a fool, for wise men know well enough what monsters° you make of them. To a nunnery, go, and quickly too. Farewell.

Ophelia. Heavenly powers, restore him!

Hamlet. I have heard of your paintings, well enough.
145　God hath given you one face, and you make your-selves another. You jig and amble, and you lisp; you nickname God's creatures and make your wantonness your ignorance.° Go to, I'll no more on't; it hath made me mad. I say we will have no
150　moe° marriage. Those that are married already—all but one—shall live. The rest shall keep as they are. To a nunnery, go.　　　　　　　　　　　　*Exit.*

Ophelia. O what a noble mind is here o'erthrown! The courtier's, soldier's, scholar's, eye, tongue, sword,
155　Th' expectancy and rose° of the fair state, The glass of fashion, and the mold of form,° Th' observed of all observers, quite, quite down! And I, of ladies most deject and wretched, That sucked the honey of his musicked vows,
160　Now see that noble and most sovereign reason Like sweet bells jangled, out of time and harsh, That unmatched form and feature of blown° youth Blasted with ecstasy.° O, woe is me T' have seen what I have seen, see what I see!

Enter King and Polonius.

141 **monsters** horned beasts, cuckolds　147–48 **make your wantonness your ignorance** excuse your wanton speech by pretending ignorance　150 **moe** more　155 **expectancy and rose** i.e., fair hope　156 **The glass ... of form** the mirror of fashion, and the pattern of excellent behavior　162 **blown** blooming　163 **ecstasy** madness

King. Love? His affections° do not that way tend,   *165*
 Nor what he spake, though it lacked form a little,
 Was not like madness. There's something in his soul
 O'er which his melancholy sits on brood,
 And I do doubt° the hatch and the disclose
 Will be some danger; which for to prevent,   *170*
 I have in quick determination
 Thus set it down: he shall with speed to England
 For the demand of our neglected tribute.
 Haply the seas, and countries different,
 With variable objects, shall expel   *175*
 This something-settled° matter in his heart,
 Whereon his brains still beating puts him thus
 From fashion of himself. What think you on't?

Polonius. It shall do well. But yet do I believe
 The origin and commencement of his grief   *180*
 Sprung from neglected love. How now, Ophelia?
 You need not tell us what Lord Hamlet said;
 We heard it all. My lord, do as you please,
 But if you hold it fit, after the play,
 Let his queen mother all alone entreat him   *185*
 To show his grief. Let her be round° with him,
 And I'll be placed, so please you, in the ear
 Of all their conference. If she find him not,°
 To England send him, or confine him where
 Your wisdom best shall think.

King.   It shall be so.   *190*
 Madness in great ones must not unwatched go.
           Exeunt.

---

165 **affections** inclinations   169 **doubt** fear   176 **something-settled** somewhat settled   186 **round** blunt   188 **find him not** does not find him out.

[Scene 2. *The castle.*]

Enter Hamlet and three of the Players.

Hamlet. Speak the speech, I pray you, as I pronounced
it to you, trippingly on the tongue. But if you mouth
it, as many of our players do, I had as lief the town
crier spoke my lines. Nor do not saw the air too much
5   with your hand, thus, but use all gently, for in the
very torrent, tempest, and (as I may say) whirlwind
of your passion, you must acquire and beget a tem-
perance that may give it smoothness. O, it offends
me to the soul to hear a robustious periwig-pated°
10   fellow tear a passion to tatters, to very rags, to split
the ears of the groundlings,° who for the most part
are capable of° nothing but inexplicable dumb
shows° and noise. I would have such a fellow
whipped for o'erdoing Termagant. It out-herods
15   Herod.° Pray you avoid it.

Player. I warrant your honor.

Hamlet. Be not too tame neither, but let your own discretion be your tutor. Suit the action to the word, the
word to the action, with this special observance, that
20   you o'erstep not the modesty of nature. For anything
so o'erdone is from° the purpose of playing, whose
end, both at the first and now, was and is, to hold,
as 'twere, the mirror up to nature; to show virtue
her own feature, scorn her own image, and the very
25   age and body of the time his form and pressure.°

3.2.9 **robustious periwig-pated** boisterous wig-headed   11 **groundlings** those who stood in the pit of the theater (the poorest and presumably most ignorant of the audience)   12 **are capable of** are able to
understand   12–13 **dumb shows** (it had been the fashion for actors
to preface plays or parts of plays with silent mime)   14–15 **Termagant ... Herod** (boisterous characters in the old mystery plays)
21 **from** contrary to   25 **pressure** image, impress

Now, this overdone, or come tardy off, though it
makes the unskillful laugh, cannot but make the
judicious grieve, the censure of the which one must
in your allowance o'erweigh a whole theater of
others. O, there be players that I have seen play,   *30*
and heard others praise, and that highly (not to
speak it profanely), that neither having th' accent of
Christians, nor the gait of Christian, pagan, nor
man, have so strutted and bellowed that I have
thought some of Nature's journeymen° had made   *35*
men, and not made them well, they imitated human-
ity so abominably.

Player. I hope we have reformed that indifferently°
with us, sir.

Hamlet. O, reform it altogether! And let those that   *40*
play your clowns speak no more than is set down
for them, for there be of them that will themselves
laugh, to set on some quantity of barren spectators to
laugh too, though in the meantime some necessary
question of the play be then to be considered. That's   *45*
villainous and shows a most pitiful ambition in the
fool that uses it. Go make you ready.

                                        Exit Players.
    Enter Polonius, Guildenstern, and Rosencrantz.

How now, my lord? Will the King hear this piece of
work?

Polonius. And the Queen too, and that presently.   *50*

Hamlet. Bid the players make haste.   *Exit Polonius.*
Will you two help to hasten them?

Rosencrantz. Ay, my lord.   *Exeunt they two.*

Hamlet. What, ho, Horatio!

                    Enter Horatio.

Horatio. Here, sweet lord, at your service.   *55*

Hamlet. Horatio, thou art e'en as just a man

35 **journeymen** workers not yet masters of their craft   38 **indifferently**
tolerably

As e'er my conversation coped withal.°

Horatio. O, my dear lord——

Hamlet.   Nay, do not think I flatter.
    For what advancement° may I hope from thee,
60   That no revenue hast but thy good spirits
    To feed and clothe thee? Why should the poor be
      flattered?
    No, let the candied° tongue lick absurd pomp,
    And crook the pregnant° hinges of the knee
    Where thrift° may follow fawning. Dost thou hear?
65   Since my dear soul was mistress of her choice
    And could of men distinguish her election,
    S' hath sealed thee° for herself, for thou hast been
    As one, in suff'ring all, that suffers nothing,°
    A man that Fortune's buffets and rewards
70   Hast ta'en with equal thanks; and blest are those
    Whose blood° and judgment are so well com-
      meddled°
    That they are not a pipe for Fortune's finger
    To sound what stop she please. Give me that man
    That is not passion's slave, and I will wear him
75   In my heart's core, ay, in my heart of heart,
    As I do thee. Something too much of this—
    There is a play tonight before the King.
    One scene of it comes near the circumstance
    Which I have told thee, of my father's death.
80   I prithee, when thou seest that act afoot,
    Even with the very comment° of thy soul
    Observe my uncle. If his occulted° guilt
    Do not itself unkennel in one speech,
    It is a damnèd ghost that we have seen,
85   And my imaginations are as foul
    As Vulcan's stithy.° Give him heedful note,
    For I mine eyes will rivet to his face,

57 **coped withal** met with 59 **advancement** promotion 62 **candied** sugared, flattering 63 **pregnant** (1) pliant (2) full of promise of good fortune 64 **thrift** profit 67 **S' hath sealed thee** she (the soul) has set a mark on you 68 **As one ... nothing** Shakespeare puns on *suffering*: Horatio *undergoes* all things, but is *harmed* by none 71 **blood** passion 71 **commeddled** blended 81 **very comment** deepest wisdom 82 **occulted** hidden 86 **stithy** forge, smithy

And after we will both our judgments join
In censure of his seeming.°

Horatio.   Well, my lord.
If 'a steal aught the whilst this play is playing,   90
And scape detecting, I will pay the theft.

*Enter Trumpets and Kettledrums, King, Queen,
Polonius, Ophelia, Rosencrantz, Guildenstern,
and other Lords attendant with his Guard carrying
torches. Danish March. Sound a Flourish.*

Hamlet. They are coming to the play: I must be idle;°
Get you a place.

King. How fares our cousin Hamlet?

Hamlet. Excellent, i' faith, of the chameleon's dish;°   95
I eat the air, promise-crammed; you cannot feed
capons so.

King. I have nothing with this answer, Hamlet; these
words are not mine.

Hamlet. No, nor mine now. [*To Polonius*] My lord, you   101
played once i' th' university, you say?

Polonius. That did I, my lord, and was accounted a good
actor.

Hamlet. What did you enact?

Polonius. I did enact Julius Caesar. I was killed i' th'   105
Capitol; Brutus killed me.

Hamlet. It was a brute part of him to kill so capital a
calf there. Be the players ready?

Rosencrantz. Ay, my lord. They stay upon your patience.   110

Queen. Come hither, my dear Hamlet, sit by me.

Hamlet. No, good mother. Here's metal more attractive.°

---

89 **censure of his seeming** judgment on his looks   92 **be idle** play the
fool   95 **the chameleon's dish** air (on which chameleons were thought
to live)   112–13 **attractive** magnetic

Polonius. [*To the King*] O ho! Do you mark that?

115   *Hamlet.* Lady, shall I lie in your lap?

  [*He lies at Ophelia's feet.*]

Ophelia. No, my lord.

Hamlet. I mean, my head upon your lap?

Ophelia. Ay, my lord.

Hamlet. Do you think I meant country matters?°

120   *Ophelia.* I think nothing, my lord.

Hamlet. That's a fair thought to lie between maids' legs.

Ophelia. What is, my lord?

Hamlet. Nothing.

125   *Ophelia.* You are merry, my lord.

Hamlet. Who, I?

Ophelia. Ay, my lord.

Hamlet. O God, your only jig-maker!° What should a
  man do but be merry? For look you how cheerfully
130   my mother looks, and my father died within's two
  hours.

Ophelia. Nay, 'tis twice two months, my lord.

Hamlet. So long? Nay then, let the devil wear black,
  for I'll have a suit of sables.° O heavens! Die two
135   months ago, and not forgotten yet? Then there's
  hope a great man's memory may outlive his life half
  a year. But, by'r Lady, 'a must build churches then,
  or else shall 'a suffer not thinking on, with the hobbyhorse,° whose epitaph is "For O, for O, the hobby-
140   horse is forgot!"

The trumpets sound. Dumb show follows:

119 **country matters** rustic doings (with a pun on the vulgar word for
the pudendum)   128 **jig-maker** composer of songs and dances (often a
Fool, who performed them)   134 **sables** (pun on "black" and "luxurious
furs")   138–39 **hobbyhorse** mock horse worn by a performer in the
morris dance

Enter a King and a Queen very lovingly, the Queen em-
bracing him, and he her. She kneels; and makes show
of protestation unto him. He takes her up, and declines
his head upon her neck. He lies him down upon a bank
of flowers. She, seeing him asleep, leaves him. Anon
come in another man: takes off his crown, kisses it,
pours poison in the sleeper's ears, and leaves him. The
Queen returns, finds the King dead, makes passionate
action. The poisoner, with some three or four, come in
again, seem to condole with her. The dead body is car-
ried away. The poisoner woos the Queen with gifts; she
seems harsh awhile, but in the end accepts love.

                                        Exeunt.

Ophelia. What means this, my lord?

Hamlet. Marry, this is miching mallecho;° it means
  mischief.

Ophelia. Belike this show imports the argument° of
  the play.   *145*

                    Enter Prologue.

Hamlet. We shall know by this fellow. The players
  cannot keep counsel; they'll tell all.

Ophelia. Will 'a tell us what this show meant?

Hamlet. Ay, or any show that you will show him. Be
  not you ashamed to show, he'll not shame to tell you   *150*
  what it means.

Ophelia. You are naught,° you are naught; I'll mark
  the play.

Prologue. For us, and for our tragedy,
        Here stooping to your clemency,   *155*
        We beg your hearing patiently.   [*Exit.*]

Hamlet. Is this a prologue, or the posy of a ring?°

Ophelia. 'Tis brief, my lord.

Hamlet. As woman's love.

142 **miching mallecho** sneaking mischief   144 **argument** plot
152 **naught** wicked, improper   157 **posy of a ring** motto inscribed in
a ring.

Enter [two Players as] King and Queen.

Player King. Full thirty times hath Phoebus' cart° gone
160   round
        Neptune's salt wash° and Tellus'° orbèd ground,
        And thirty dozen moons with borrowed sheen
        About the world have times twelve thirties been,
        Since love our hearts, and Hymen did our hands,
165   Unite commutual in most sacred bands.

Player Queen. So many journeys may the sun and
            moon
        Make us again count o'er ere love be done!
        But woe is me, you are so sick of late,
        So far from cheer and from your former state,
170   That I distrust° you. Yet, though I distrust,
        Discomfort you, my lord, it nothing must.
        For women fear too much, even as they love,
        And women's fear and love hold quantity,
        In neither aught, or in extremity.°
175   Now what my love is, proof° hath made you know,
        And as my love is sized, my fear is so.
        Where love is great, the littlest doubts are fear;
        Where little fears grow great, great love grows there.

Player King. Faith, I must leave thee, love, and shortly
            too;
180   My operant° powers their functions leave to do:
        And thou shalt live in this fair world behind,
        Honored, beloved, and haply one as kind
        For husband shalt thou——

Player Queen.   O, confound the rest!
        Such love must needs be treason in my breast.
185   In second husband let me be accurst!
        None wed the second but who killed the first.

160 **Phoebus' cart** the sun's chariot   161 **Neptune's salt wash** the sea
161 **Tellus** Roman goddess of the earth   170 **distrust** am anxious
about   173–74 **And women's . . . in extremity** (perhaps the idea is that
women's anxiety is great or little in proportion to their love. The previous line, unrhymed, may be a false start that Shakespeare neglected to
delete)   175 **proof** experience   180 **operant** active

Hamlet. [Aside] That's wormwood.°

Player Queen. The instances° that second marriage
 move°
Are base respects of thrift,° but none of love.
A second time I kill my husband dead   *190*
When second husband kisses me in bed.

Player King. I do believe you think what now you
 speak,
But what we do determine oft we break.
Purpose is but the slave to memory,
Of violent birth, but poor validity,°   *195*
Which now like fruit unripe sticks on the tree,
But fall unshaken when they mellow be.
Most necessary 'tis that we forget
To pay ourselves what to ourselves is debt.
What to ourselves in passion we propose,   *200*
The passion ending, doth the purpose lose.
The violence of either grief or joy
Their own enactures° with themselves destroy:
Where joy most revels, grief doth most lament;
Grief joys, joy grieves, on slender accident.   *205*
This world is not for aye, nor 'tis not strange
That even our loves should with our fortunes
 change,
For 'tis a question left us yet to prove,
Whether love lead fortune, or else fortune love.
The great man down, you mark his favorite flies;   *210*
The poor advanced makes friends of enemies;
And hitherto doth love on fortune tend,
For who not needs shall never lack a friend;
And who in want a hollow friend doth try,
Directly seasons him° his enemy.   *215*
But, orderly to end where I begun,
Our wills and fates do so contrary run
That our devices still are overthrown;
Our thoughts are ours, their ends none of our own.

187 **wormwood** a bitter herb   188 **instances** motives   188 **move** in-
duce   189 **respects of thrift** considerations of profit   195 **validity**
strength   203 **enactures** acts   215 **seasons him** ripens him into

220   So think thou wilt no second husband wed,
        But die thy thoughts when thy first lord is dead.

        Player Queen. Nor earth to me give food, nor heaven
            light,
        Sport and repose lock from me day and night,
        To desperation turn my trust and hope,
225   An anchor's° cheer in prison be my scope,
        Each opposite that blanks° the face of joy
        Meet what I would have well, and it destroy:
        Both here and hence pursue me lasting strife,
        If, once a widow, ever I be wife!

230   *Hamlet.* If she should break it now!

        Player King. 'Tis deeply sworn. Sweet, leave me here
            awhile;
        My spirits grow dull, and fain I would beguile
        The tedious day with sleep.

        Player Queen.   Sleep rock thy brain,
                                           [*He*] *sleeps.*
        And never come mischance between us twain!   *Exit.*

235   *Hamlet.* Madam, how like you this play?

        Queen. The lady doth protest too much, methinks.

        Hamlet. O, but she'll keep her word.

        King. Have you heard the argument?° Is there no
        offense in't?

240   *Hamlet.* No, no, they do but jest, poison in jest; no
        offense i' th' world.

        King. What do you call the play?

        Hamlet. The Mousetrap. Marry, how? Tropically.°
        This play is the image of a murder done in Vienna:
245   Gonzago is the Duke's name; his wife, Baptista. You
        shall see anon. 'Tis a knavish piece of work, but
        what of that? Your Majesty, and we that have free°

        ---

        225 **anchor's** anchorite's, hermit's   226 **opposite that blanks** adverse
        thing that blanches   238 **argument** plot   243 **Tropically** figuratively
        (with a pun on "trap")   247 **free** innocent

souls, it touches us not. Let the galled jade winch;°
our withers are unwrung.

Enter Lucianus.

This is one Lucianus, nephew to the King. 250

Ophelia. You are as good as a chorus, my lord.

Hamlet. I could interpret° between you and your love,
  if I could see the puppets dallying.

Ophelia. You are keen,° my lord, you are keen.

Hamlet. It would cost you a groaning to take off mine 255
  edge.

Ophelia. Still better, and worse.

Hamlet. So you mistake° your husbands.—Begin,
  murderer. Leave thy damnable faces and begin.
  Come, the croaking raven doth bellow for revenge. 260

Lucianus. Thoughts black, hands apt, drugs fit, and
    time agreeing,
  Confederate season,° else no creature seeing,
  Thou mixture rank, of midnight weeds collected,
  With Hecate's ban° thrice blasted, thrice infected,
  Thy natural magic and dire property° 265
  On wholesome life usurps immediately.

Pours the poison in his ears.

Hamlet. 'A poisons him i' th' garden for his estate. His
  name's Gonzago. The story is extant, and written in
  very choice Italian. You shall see anon how the murderer gets the love of Gonzago's wife. 270

Ophelia. The King rises.

Hamlet. What, frighted with false fire?°

Queen. How fares my lord?

Polonius. Give o'er the play.

---

248 **galled jade winch** chafed horse wince   252 **interpret** (like a show-
man explaining the action of puppets)   254 **keen** (1) sharp (2) sexually
aroused   258 **mistake** err in taking   262 **Confederate season** the op-
portunity allied with me   264 **Hecate's ban** the curse of the goddess of
sorcery   265 **property** nature   272 **false fire** blank discharge of
firearms

275 *King.* Give me some light. Away!

Polonius. Lights, lights, lights!

Exeunt all but Hamlet and Horatio.

Hamlet. Why, let the strucken deer go weep,
      The hart ungallèd play:
   For some must watch, while some must sleep;

280   Thus runs the world away.
   Would not this, sir, and a forest of feathers°—if the
   rest of my fortunes turn Turk° with me—with two
   Provincial roses° on my razed° shoes, get me a
   fellowship in a cry° of players?

285 *Horatio.* Half a share.

Hamlet. A whole one, I.
      For thou dost know, O Damon dear,
      This realm dismantled was
   Of Jove himself; and now reigns here

290   A very, very—pajock.°

Horatio. You might have rhymed.°

Hamlet. O good Horatio, I'll take the ghost's word for
   a thousand pound. Didst perceive?

Horatio. Very well, my lord.

295 *Hamlet.* Upon the talk of poisoning?

Horatio. I did very well note him.

Hamlet. Ah ha! Come, some music! Come, the recorders!°
      For if the King like not the comedy,

300   Why then, belike he likes it not, perdy.°
   Come, some music!

Enter Rosencrantz and Guildenstern.

Guildenstern. Good my lord, vouchsafe me a word
   with you.

---

281 **feathers** (plumes were sometimes part of a costume)   282 **turn Turk** i.e., go bad, treat me badly   283 **Provincial roses** rosettes like the roses of Provence (?)   283 **razed** ornamented with slashes   284 **cry** pack, company   290 **pajock** peacock   291 **You might have rhymed** i.e., rhymed "was" with "ass"   297–98 **recorders** flutelike instruments
300 **perdy** by God (French: *par dieu*)

Hamlet. Sir, a whole history.

Guildenstern. The King, sir—— 305

Hamlet. Ay, sir, what of him?

Guildenstern. Is in his retirement marvelous distemp'red.

Hamlet. With drink, sir?

Guildenstern. No, my lord, with choler.° 310

Hamlet. Your wisdom should show itself more richer to signify this to the doctor, for for me to put him to his purgation would perhaps plunge him into more choler.

Guildenstern. Good my lord, put your discourse into 315 some frame,° and start not so wildly from my affair.

Hamlet. I am tame, sir; pronounce.

Guildenstern. The Queen, your mother, in most great affliction of spirit hath sent me to you.

Hamlet. You are welcome. 320

Guildenstern. Nay, good my lord, this courtesy is not of the right breed. If it shall please you to make me a wholesome answer, I will do your mother's commandment: if not, your pardon and my return shall be the end of my business. 325

Hamlet. Sir, I cannot.

Rosencrantz. What, my lord?

Hamlet. Make you a wholesome° answer; my wit's diseased. But, sir, such answer as I can make, you shall command, or rather, as you say, my mother. 330 Therefore no more, but to the matter. My mother, you say——

Rosencrantz. Then thus she says: your behavior hath struck her into amazement and admiration.°

310 **choler** anger (but Hamlet pretends to take the word in its sense of "biliousness") 316 **frame** order, control 328 **wholesome** sane 334 **admiration** wonder

335 *Hamlet.* O wonderful son, that can so stonish a mother!
But is there no sequel at the heels of this mother's
admiration? Impart.

Rosencrantz. She desires to speak with you in her
closet ere you go to bed.

340 *Hamlet.* We shall obey, were she ten times our mother.
Have you any further trade with us?

Rosencrantz. My lord, you once did love me.

Hamlet. And do still, by these pickers and stealers.°

Rosencrantz. Good my lord, what is your cause of dis-
345 temper? You do surely bar the door upon your own
liberty, if you deny your griefs to your friend.

Hamlet. Sir, I lack advancement.°

Rosencrantz. How can that be, when you have the
voice of the King himself for your succession in
350 Denmark?

Enter the Players with recorders.

Hamlet. Ay, sir, but "while the grass grows"—the
proverb° is something musty. O, the recorders. Let
me see one. To withdraw° with you—why do you
go about to recover the wind° of me as if you would
355 drive me into a toil?°

Guildenstern. O my lord, if my duty be too bold, my
love is too unmannerly.°

Hamlet. I do not well understand that. Will you play
upon this pipe?

360 *Guildenstern.* My lord, I cannot.

Hamlet. I pray you.

Guildenstern. Believe me, I cannot.

Hamlet. I pray you.

Guildenstern. Believe me, I cannot.

343 **pickers and stealers** i.e., hands (with reference to the prayer; "Keep
my hands from picking and stealing") 347 **advancement** promotion 352 **proverb** ("While the grass groweth, the horse starveth")
353 **withdraw** speak in private 354 **recover the wind** get on the wind-
ward side (as in hunting) 355 **toil** snare 356–57 **if my duty ... too
unmannerly** i.e., if these questions seem rude, it is because my love for
you leads me beyond good manners.

Hamlet. I do beseech you.

Guildenstern. I know no touch of it, my lord.

Hamlet. It is as easy as lying. Govern these ventages° 365
with your fingers and thumb, give it breath with your
mouth, and it will discourse most eloquent music.
Look you, these are the stops.

Guildenstern. But these cannot I command to any
utt'rance of harmony; I have not the skill. 370

Hamlet. Why, look you now, how unworthy a thing
you make of me! You would play upon me; you
would seem to know my stops; you would pluck
out the heart of my mystery; you would sound me
from my lowest note to the top of my compass;° 375
and there is much music, excellent voice, in this little
organ,° yet cannot you make it speak. 'Sblood, do
you think I am easier to be played on than a pipe?
Call me what instrument you will, though you can
fret° me, you cannot play upon me. 380

Enter Polonius.

God bless you, sir!

Polonius. My lord, the Queen would speak with you,
and presently.

Hamlet. Do you see yonder cloud that's almost in
shape of a camel? 385

Polonius. By th' mass and 'tis, like a camel indeed.

Hamlet. Methinks it is like a weasel.

Polonius. It is backed like a weasel.

Hamlet. Or like a whale.

Polonius. Very like a whale. 390

Hamlet. Then I will come to my mother by and by.

---

365 **ventages** vents, stops on a recorder   375 **compass** range of voice
377 **organ** i.e., the recorder   380 **fret** vex (with a pun alluding to the
frets, or ridges, that guide the fingering on some stringed instruments)

[*Aside*] They fool me to the top of my bent.°—I
will come by and by.°

Polonius. I will say so.   *Exit.*

395 *Hamlet.* "By and by" is easily said. Leave me, friends.
                         [*Exeunt all but Hamlet.*]
'Tis now the very witching time of night,
When churchyards yawn, and hell itself breathes out
Contagion to this world. Now could I drink hot
    blood
And do such bitter business as the day
400 Would quake to look on. Soft, now to my mother.
O heart, lose not thy nature; let not ever
The soul of Nero° enter this firm bosom.
Let me be cruel, not unnatural;
I will speak daggers to her, but use none.
405 My tongue and soul in this be hypocrites:
How in my words somever she be shent,°
To give them seals° never, my soul, consent!   *Exit.*

[Scene 3. *The castle.*]

Enter King, Rosencrantz, and Guildenstern.

King. I like him not, nor stands it safe with us
To let his madness range. Therefore prepare you.
I your commission will forthwith dispatch,
And he to England shall along with you.
5   The terms° of our estate may not endure
Hazard so near's° as doth hourly grow
Out of his brows.

Guildenstern.   We will ourselves provide.

---

392 **They fool ... my bent** they compel me to play the fool to the
limit of my capacity   393 **by and by** very soon   402 **Nero** (Roman
emperor who had his mother murdered)   406 **shent** rebuked   407 **give
them seals** confirm them with deeds   3.3.5 **terms** conditions   6 **near's**
near us

Most holy and religious fear it is
To keep those many many bodies safe
That live and feed upon your Majesty.   *10*

Rosencrantz. The single and peculiar° life is bound
With all the strength and armor of the mind
To keep itself from noyance,° but much more
That spirit upon whose weal depends and rests
The lives of many. The cess of majesty°   *15*
Dies not alone, but like a gulf° doth draw
What's near it with it; or it is a massy wheel
Fixed on the summit of the highest mount,
To whose huge spokes ten thousand lesser things
Are mortised and adjoined, which when it falls,   *20*
Each small annexment, petty consequence,
Attends° the boist'rous ruin. Never alone
Did the King sigh, but with a general groan.

King. Arm° you, I pray you, to this speedy voyage,
For we will fetters put about this fear,   *25*
Which now goes too free-footed.

Rosencrantz.   We will haste us.
                              Exeunt Gentlemen.

                    Enter Polonius.

Polonius. My lord, he's going to his mother's closet.°
Behind the arras I'll convey myself
To hear the process.° I'll warrant she'll tax him
    home,°
And, as you said, and wisely was it said,   *30*
'Tis meet that some more audience than a mother,
Since nature makes them partial, should o'erhear
The speech of vantage.° Fare you well, my liege.
I'll call upon you ere you go to bed
And tell you what I know.

King.   Thanks, dear my lord.   *35*
                        Exit [Polonius].

11 **peculiar** individual, private   13 **noyance** injury   15 **cess of majesty** cessation (death) of a king   16 **gulf** whirlpool   22 **Attends** waits on, participates in   24 **Arm** prepare   27 **closet** private room   29 **process** proceedings   29 **tax him home** censure him sharply   33 **of vantage** from an advantageous place

O, my offense is rank, it smells to heaven;
It hath the primal eldest curse° upon't,
A brother's murder. Pray can I not,
Though inclination be as sharp as will.
40 My stronger guilt defeats my strong intent,
And like a man to double business bound
I stand in pause where I shall first begin,
And both neglect. What if this cursèd hand
Were thicker than itself with brother's blood,
45 Is there not rain enough in the sweet heavens
To wash it white as snow? Whereto serves mercy
But to confront° the visage of offense?
And what's in prayer but this twofold force,
To be forestallèd ere we come to fall,
50 Or pardoned being down? Then I'll look up.
My fault is past. But, O, what form of prayer
Can serve my turn? "Forgive me my foul murder"?
That cannot be, since I am still possessed
Of those effects° for which I did the murder,
55 My crown, mine own ambition, and my queen.
May one be pardoned and retain th' offense?
In the corrupted currents of this world
Offense's gilded hand may shove by justice,
And oft 'tis seen the wicked prize itself
60 Buys out the law. But 'tis not so above.
There is no shuffling;° there the action lies
In his true nature, and we ourselves compelled,
Even to the teeth and forehead of our faults,
To give in evidence. What then? What rests?°
65 Try what repentance can. What can it not?
Yet what can it when one cannot repent?
O wretched state! O bosom black as death!
O limèd° soul, that struggling to be free
Art more engaged!° Help, angels! Make assay.°
70 Bow, stubborn knees, and, heart with strings of steel,

---

37 **primal eldest curse** (curse of Cain, who killed Abel)   47 **confront**
oppose   54 **effects** things gained   61 **shuffling** trickery   64 **rests** remains   68 **limèd** caught (as with birdlime, a sticky substance spread on
boughs to snare birds)   69 **engaged** ensnared   69 **assay** an attempt

> Be soft as sinews of the newborn babe.
> All may be well.   [*He kneels.*]

Enter Hamlet.

Hamlet. Now might I do it pat, now 'a is a-praying,
And now I'll do't. And so 'a goes to heaven,
And so am I revenged. That would be scanned.°   75
A villain kills my father, and for that
I, his sole son, do this same villain send
To heaven.
Why, this is hire and salary, not revenge.
'A took my father grossly, full of bread,°   80
With all his crimes broad blown,° as flush° as May;
And how his audit° stands, who knows save heaven?
But in our circumstance and course of thought,
'Tis heavy with him; and am I then revenged,
To take him in the purging of his soul,   85
When he is fit and seasoned for his passage?
No.
Up, sword, and know thou a more horrid hent.°
When he is drunk asleep, or in his rage,
Or in th' incestuous pleasure of his bed,   90
At game a-swearing, or about some act
That has no relish° of salvation in't—
Then trip him, that his heels may kick at heaven,
And that his soul may be as damned and black
As hell, whereto it goes. My mother stays.   95
This physic° but prolongs thy sickly days.   *Exit.*

King. [*Rises*] My words fly up, my thoughts remain
below.
Words without thoughts never to heaven go.   *Exit.*

---

75 **would be scanned** ought to be looked into   80 **bread** i. e., worldly gratification   81 **crimes broad blown** sins in full bloom   81 **flush** vigorous   82 **audit** account   88 **hent** grasp (here, occasion for seizing)   92 **relish** flavor   96 **physic** (Claudius' purgation by prayer, as Hamlet thinks in line 85)

[Scene 4. *The Queen's private chamber.*]

Enter [Queen] Gertrude and Polonius.

Polonius. 'A will come straight. Look you lay home°
　to him.
　Tell him his pranks have been too broad° to bear
　with,
　And that your Grace hath screened and stood be-
　tween
　Much heat and him. I'll silence me even here.
5　Pray you be round with him.

Hamlet. (*Within*) Mother, Mother, Mother!

Queen. I'll warrant you; fear me not. Withdraw; I hear
　him coming.　　　[*Polonius hides behind the arras.*]

Enter Hamlet.

Hamlet. Now, Mother, what's the matter?

10　*Queen.* Hamlet, thou hast thy father much offended.

Hamlet. Mother, you have my father much offended.

Queen. Come, come, you answer with an idle° tongue.

Hamlet. Go, go, you question with a wicked tongue.

Queen. Why, how now, Hamlet?

Hamlet.　　　　　　　　　　What's the matter now?

Queen. Have you forgot me?

15　*Hamlet.*　　　　　　　　No, by the rood,° not so!
　You are the Queen, your husband's brother's wife,
　And, would it were not so, you are my mother.

Queen. Nay, then I'll set those to you that can speak.

Hamlet. Come, come, and sit you down. You shall not
　budge.

3.4.1 **lay home** thrust (rebuke) him sharply　2 **broad** unrestrained
12 **idle** foolish　15 **rood** cross

You go not till I set you up a glass°   20
Where you may see the inmost part of you!

Queen. What wilt thou do? Thou wilt not murder me?
Help, ho!

Polonius. [*Behind*] What, ho! Help!

Hamlet. [*Draws*] How now? A rat? Dead for a ducat,
dead!   25
[*Thrusts his rapier through the arras and*] *kills Polonius.*

Polonius. [*Behind*] O, I am slain!

Queen.   O me, what hast thou done?

Hamlet. Nay, I know not. Is it the King?

Queen. O, what a rash and bloody deed is this!

Hamlet. A bloody deed—almost as bad, good Mother,
As kill a king, and marry with his brother.   30

Queen. As kill a king?

Hamlet.   Ay, lady, it was my word.
                    [*Lifts up the arras and sees Polonius.*]
Thou wretched, rash, intruding fool, farewell!
I took thee for thy better. Take thy fortune.
Thou find'st to be too busy is some danger.—
Leave wringing of your hands. Peace, sit you down   35
And let me wring your heart, for so I shall
If it be made of penetrable stuff,
If damnèd custom have not brazed° it so
That it be proof° and bulwark against sense.°

Queen. What have I done that thou dar'st wag thy
tongue   40
In noise so rude against me?

Hamlet.   Such an act
That blurs the grace and blush of modesty,
Calls virtue hypocrite, takes off the rose
From the fair forehead of an innocent love,
And sets a blister° there, makes marriage vows   45

---

20 **glass** mirror   38 **brazed** hardened like brass   39 **proof** armor
39 **sense** feeling   45 **sets a blister** brands (as a harlot)

As false as dicers' oaths. O, such a deed
As from the body of contraction° plucks
The very soul, and sweet religion makes
A rhapsody° of words! Heaven's face does glow
50 O'er this solidity and compound mass
With heated visage, as against the doom
Is thoughtsick at the act.°

Queen.   Ay me, what act,
That roars so loud and thunders in the index?°

Hamlet. Look here upon this picture, and on this,
55 The counterfeit presentment° of two brothers.
See what a grace was seated on this brow:
Hyperion's curls, the front° of Jove himself,
An eye like Mars, to threaten and command,
A station° like the herald Mercury
60 New lighted on a heaven-kissing hill—
A combination and a form indeed
Where every god did seem to set his seal
To give the world assurance of a man.
This was your husband. Look you now what follows.
65 Here is your husband, like a mildewed ear
Blasting his wholesome brother. Have you eyes?
Could you on this fair mountain leave to feed,
And batten° on this moor? Ha! Have you eyes?
You cannot call it love, for at your age
70 The heyday° in the blood is tame, it's humble,
And waits upon the judgment, and what judgment
Would step from this to this? Sense° sure you have,
Else could you not have motion, but sure that sense
Is apoplexed,° for madness would not err,
75 Nor sense to ecstasy° was ne'er so thralled
But it reserved some quantity of choice

---

47 **contraction** marriage contract 49 **rhapsody** senseless string
49–52 **Heaven's face . . . the act** i.e., the face of heaven blushes over
this earth (compounded of four elements), the face hot, as if Judgment
Day were near, and it is thoughtsick at the act 53 **index** prologue 55
counterfeit presentment represented image 57 **front** forehead 59
station bearing 68 **batten** feed gluttonously 70 **heyday** excitement
72 **Sense** feeling 74 **apoplexed** paralyzed 75 **ecstasy** madness

To serve in such a difference. What devil was't
That thus hath cozened you at hoodman-blind?°
Eyes without feeling, feeling without sight,
Ears without hands or eyes, smelling sans° all,   *80*
Or but a sickly part of one true sense
Could not so mope.°
O shame, where is thy blush? Rebellious hell,
If thou canst mutine in a matron's bones,
To flaming youth let virtue be as wax   *85*
And melt in her own fire. Proclaim no shame
When the compulsive ardor° gives the charge,
Since frost itself as actively doth burn,
And reason panders will.°

Queen.   O Hamlet, speak no more.
Thou turn'st mine eyes into my very soul,   *90*
And there I see such black and grainèd° spots
As will not leave their tinct.°

Hamlet.   Nay, but to live
In the rank sweat of an enseamèd° bed,
Stewed in corruption, honeying and making love
Over the nasty sty——

Queen.   O, speak to me no more.   *95*
These words like daggers enter in my ears.
No more, sweet Hamlet.

Hamlet.   A murderer and a villain,
A slave that is not twentieth part the tithe°
Of your precedent lord, a vice° of kings,
A cutpurse of the empire and the rule,   *100*
That from a shelf the precious diadem stole
And put it in his pocket——

Queen.   No more.

---

78 **cozened you at hoodman-blind** cheated you at blindman's buff
80 **sans** without 82 **mope** be stupid 87 **compulsive ardor** com-
pelling passion 89 **reason panders will** reason acts as a procurer
for desire 91 **grainèd** dyed in grain (fast dyed) 92 **tinct** color 93
enseamèd (perhaps "soaked in grease," i.e., sweaty; perhaps "much
wrinkled") 98 **tithe** tenth part 99 **vice** (like the Vice, a fool and
mischief-maker in the old morality plays)

Enter Ghost.

Hamlet. A king of shreds and patches—
 Save me and hover o'er me with your wings,
 You heavenly guards! What would your gracious
105 figure?

Queen. Alas, he's mad.

Hamlet. Do you not come your tardy son to chide,
 That, lapsed in time and passion, lets go by
 Th' important acting of your dread command?
110 O, say!

Ghost. Do not forget. This visitation
 Is but to whet thy almost blunted purpose.
 But look, amazement on thy mother sits.
 O, step between her and her fighting soul!
115 Conceit° in weakest bodies strongest works.
 Speak to her, Hamlet.

Hamlet.   How is it with you, lady?

Queen. Alas, how is't with you,
 That you do bend your eye on vacancy,
 And with th' incorporal° air do hold discourse?
120 Forth at your eyes your spirits wildly peep,
 And as the sleeping soldiers in th' alarm
 Your bedded hair° like life in excrements°
 Start up and stand an end.° O gentle son,
 Upon the heat and flame of thy distemper
125 Sprinkle cool patience. Whereon do you look?

Hamlet. On him, on him! Look you, how pale he
  glares!
 His form and cause conjoined, preaching to stones,
 Would make them capable.°—Do not look upon
  me,
 Lest with this piteous action you convert
130 My stern effects.° Then what I have to do
 Will want true color; tears perchance for blood.

Queen. To whom do you speak this?

115 **Conceit** imagination   119 **incorporal** bodiless   122 **bedded hair**
hairs laid flat   122 **excrements** outgrowths (here, the hair)   123 **an
end** on end   128 **capable** receptive   129–30 **convert/My stern effects**
divert my stern deeds

Hamlet.   Do you see nothing there?

Queen. Nothing at all; yet all that is I see.

Hamlet. Nor did you nothing hear?

Queen.   No, nothing but ourselves.

Hamlet. Why, look you there! Look how it steals away!   *135*
   My father, in his habit° as he lived!
   Look where he goes even now out at the portal!

                                     Exit Ghost.

Queen. This is the very coinage of your brain.
   This bodiless creation ecstasy
   Is very cunning in.

Hamlet.   Ecstasy?   *140*
   My pulse as yours doth temperately keep time
   And makes as healthful music. It is not madness
   That I have uttered. Bring me to the test,
   And I the matter will reword, which madness
   Would gambol° from. Mother, for love of grace,   *145*
   Lay not that flattering unction° to your soul,
   That not your trespass but my madness speaks.
   It will but skin and film the ulcerous place
   Whiles rank corruption, mining° all within,
   Infects unseen. Confess yourself to heaven,   *150*
   Repent what's past, avoid what is to come,
   And do not spread the compost° on the weeds
   To make them ranker. Forgive me this my virtue.
   For in the fatness of these pursy° times
   Virtue itself of vice must pardon beg,   *155*
   Yea, curb° and woo for leave to do him good.

Queen. O Hamlet, thou hast cleft my heart in twain.

Hamlet. O, throw away the worser part of it,
   And live the purer with the other half.
   Good night—but go not to my uncle's bed.   *160*
   Assume a virtue, if you have it not.

136 **habit** garment (Q1, though a "bad" quarto, is probably correct in saying that at line 102 the ghost enters "in his nightgown," i.e., dressing gown) 145 **gambol** start away 146 **unction** ointment 149 **mining** undermining 152 **compost** fertilizing substance 154 **pursy** bloated 156 **curb** bow low

That monster custom, who all sense doth eat,
Of habits devil, is angel yet in this,
That to the use° of actions fair and good
165 He likewise gives a frock or livery°
That aptly is put on. Refrain tonight,
And that shall lend a kind of easiness
To the next abstinence; the next more easy;
For use almost can change the stamp of nature,
170 And either° the devil, or throw him out
With wondrous potency. Once more, good night,
And when you are desirous to be blest,
I'll blessing beg of you.—For this same lord,
I do repent; but heaven hath pleased it so,
175 To punish me with this, and this with me,
That I must be their° scourge and minister.
I will bestow° him and will answer well
The death I gave him. So again, good night.
I must be cruel only to be kind.
180 Thus bad begins, and worse remains behind.
One word more, good lady.

Queen.   What shall I do?

Hamlet. Not this, by no means, that I bid you do:
Let the bloat King tempt you again to bed,
Pinch wanton on your cheek, call you his mouse,
185 And let him, for a pair of reechy° kisses,
Or paddling in your neck with his damned fingers,
Make you to ravel° all this matter out,
That I essentially am not in madness,
But mad in craft. 'Twere good you let him know,
190 For who that's but a queen, fair, sober, wise,
Would from a paddock,° from a bat, a gib,°
Such dear concernings hide? Who would do so?
No, in despite of sense and secrecy,

---

164 **use** practice 165 **livery** characteristic garment (punning on
"habits" in line 163) 170 **either** (probably a word is missing after
either; among suggestions are "master," "curb," and "house"; but possibly *either* is a printer's error for *entertain*, i.e. "receive"; or perhaps *either* is a verb meaning "make easier") 176 **their** i.e., the heavens'
177 **bestow** stow, lodge 185 **reechy** foul (literally "smoky") 187
ravel unravel, reveal 191 **paddock** toad 191 **gib** tomcat

Unpeg the basket on the house's top,
Let the birds fly, and like the famous ape,   195
To try conclusions,° in the basket creep
And break your own neck down.

Queen. Be thou assured, if words be made of breath,
And breath of life, I have no life to breathe
What thou hast said to me.   200

Hamlet. I must to England; you know that?

Queen.   Alack,
I had forgot. 'Tis so concluded on.

Hamlet. There's letters sealed, and my two school-
fellows,
Whom I will trust as I will adders fanged,
They bear the mandate;° they must sweep my way   205
And marshal me to knavery. Let it work;
For 'tis the sport to have the enginer
Hoist with his own petar,° and 't shall go hard
But I will delve one yard below their mines
And blow them at the moon. O, 'tis most sweet   210
When in one line two crafts° directly meet.
This man shall set me packing:
I'll lug the guts into the neighbor room.
Mother, good night. Indeed, this counselor
Is now most still, most secret, and most grave,   215
Who was in life a foolish prating knave.
Come, sir, to draw toward an end with you.
Good night, Mother.
             [*Exit the Queen. Then*] *exit Hamlet, tugging in*
                                        Polonius.

---

196 **To try conclusions** to make experiments   205 **mandate** command
208 **petar** bomb   211 **crafts** (1) boats (2) acts of guile, crafty schemes

[ACT 4

Scene 1. *The castle.*]

*Enter King and Queen, with Rosencrantz and
Guildenstern.*

King. There's matter in these sighs. These profound
heaves
You must translate; 'tis fit we understand them.
Where is your son?

Queen. Bestow this place on us a little while.
          [*Exeunt Rosencrantz and Guildenstern.*]
5   Ah, mine own lord, what have I seen tonight!

King. What, Gertrude? How does Hamlet?

Queen. Mad as the sea and wind when both contend
Which is the mightier. In his lawless fit,
Behind the arras hearing something stir,
10   Whips out his rapier, cries, "A rat, a rat!"
And in this brainish apprehension° kills
The unseen good old man.

King.   O heavy deed!
It had been so with us, had we been there.
His liberty is full of threats to all,
15   To you yourself, to us, to every one.
Alas, how shall this bloody deed be answered?
It will be laid to us, whose providence°

4.1.11 **brainish apprehension** mad imagination   17 **providence** fore-
sight

94

Should have kept short, restrained, and out of haunt°
This mad young man. But so much was our love
We would not understand what was most fit,   20
But, like the owner of a foul disease,
To keep it from divulging, let it feed
Even on the pith of life. Where is he gone?

Queen. To draw apart the body he hath killed;
O'er whom his very madness, like some ore   25
Among a mineral° of metals base,
Shows itself pure. 'A weeps for what is done.

King. O Gertrude, come away!
The sun no sooner shall the mountains touch
But we will ship him hence, and this vile deed   30
We must with all our majesty and skill
Both countenance and excuse. Ho, Guildenstern!

    Enter Rosencrantz and Guildenstern.

Friends both, go join you with some further aid:
Hamlet in madness hath Polonius slain,
And from his mother's closet hath he dragged him.   35
Go seek him out; speak fair, and bring the body
Into the chapel. I pray you haste in this.
    [Exeunt Rosencrantz and Guildenstern.]
Come, Gertrude, we'll call up our wisest friends
And let them know both what we mean to do
And what's untimely done . . .°   40
Whose whisper o'er the world's diameter,
As level as the cannon to his blank°
Transports his poisoned shot, may miss our name
And hit the woundless° air. O, come away!
My soul is full of discord and dismay.   *Exeunt.*   45

---

18 **out of haunt** away from association with others   25–26 **ore/Among a mineral** vein of gold in a mine   40 **done** . . . (evidently something has dropped out of the text. Capell's conjecture, "So, haply slander," is usually printed)   42 **blank** white center of a target   44 **woundless** invulnerable

[Scene 2. *The castle.*]

Enter Hamlet.

Hamlet. Safely stowed.

Gentlemen. (Within) Hamlet! Lord Hamlet!

Hamlet. But soft, what noise? Who calls on Hamlet?
O, here they come.

Enter Rosencrantz and Guildenstern.

Rosencrantz. What have you done, my lord, with the
5   dead body?

Hamlet. Compounded it with dust, whereto 'tis kin.

Rosencrantz. Tell us where 'tis, that we may take it
thence
And bear it to the chapel.

Hamlet. Do not believe it.

10   *Rosencrantz.* Believe what?

Hamlet. That I can keep your counsel and not mine
own. Besides, to be demanded of° a sponge, what
replication° should be made by the son of a king?

Rosencrantz. Take you me for a sponge, my lord?

15   *Hamlet.* Ay, sir, that soaks up the King's countenance,°
his rewards, his authorities. But such officers do the
King best service in the end. He keeps them, like an
ape, in the corner of his jaw, first mouthed, to be
last swallowed. When he needs what you have
20   gleaned, it is but squeezing you and, sponge, you
shall be dry again.

Rosencrantz. I understand you not, my lord.

Hamlet. I am glad of it: a knavish speech sleeps in a
foolish ear.

4.2.12 **demanded of** questioned by   13 **replication** reply   15 **countenance** favor

Rosencrantz. My lord, you must tell us where the body   25
is and go with us to the King.

Hamlet. The body is with the King, but the King is not
with the body.° The King is a thing——

Guildenstern. A thing, my lord?

Hamlet. Of nothing. Bring me to him. Hide fox, and   30
all after.°   *Exeunt.*

[Scene 3. *The castle.*]

Enter King, and two or three.

King. I have sent to seek him and to find the body:
How dangerous is it that this man goes loose!
Yet must not we put the strong law on him:
He's loved of the distracted° multitude,
Who like not in their judgment, but their eyes,
And where 'tis so, th' offender's scourge is weighed,
But never the offense. To bear° all smooth and even,   5
This sudden sending him away must seem
Deliberate pause.° Diseases desperate grown
By desperate appliance are relieved,
Or not at all.

Enter Rosencrantz, [Guildenstern,] and all the rest.   10

How now? What hath befall'n?

Rosencrantz. Where the dead body is bestowed, my
lord,
We cannot get from him.

King.   But where is he?

Rosencrantz. Without, my lord; guarded, to know your
pleasure.

27–28 **The body . . . the body** (an allusion to a contemporary theory of
kingship that distinguished between the king's two bodies, the Body
Natural and the Body Politic. The king [Claudius] has a body, but the
Body Politic [the kingship of Denmark] is not inherent in that body)
30–31 **Hide fox, and all after** (a cry in a game such as hide-
and-seek; Hamlet runs from the stage)   4.3.4 **distracted** bewildered,
senseless   7 **bear** carry out   9 **pause** planning

King. Bring him before us.

15 *Rosencrantz.*   Ho! Bring in the lord.

                              They enter.

King. Now, Hamlet, where's Polonius?

Hamlet. At supper.

King. At supper? Where?

Hamlet. Not where he eats, but where 'a is eaten. A
20   certain convocation of politic° worms are e'en at
        him. Your worm is your only emperor for diet. We
        fat all creatures else to fat us, and we fat ourselves
        for maggots. Your fat king and your lean beggar is
        but variable service°—two dishes, but to one table.
25   That's the end.

King. Alas, alas!

Hamlet. A man may fish with the worm that hath eat of
        a king, and eat of the fish that hath fed of that worm.

King. What dost thou mean by this?

30 *Hamlet.* Nothing but to show you how a king may
        go a progress° through the guts of a beggar.

King. Where is Polonius?

Hamlet. In heaven. Send thither to see. If your mes-
        senger find him not there, seek him i' th' other
35   place yourself. But if indeed you find him not
        within this month, you shall nose him as you go
        up the stairs into the lobby.

King. [*To Attendants*] Go seek him there.

Hamlet. 'A will stay till you come.

                              [*Exeunt Attendants.*]

40 *King.* Hamlet, this deed, for thine especial safety,
        Which we do tender° as we dearly grieve
        For that which thou hast done, must send thee hence
        With fiery quickness. Therefore prepare thyself.

---

20 **politic** statesmanlike, shrewd   24 **variable service** different courses
31 **progress** royal journey   41 **tender** hold dear

The bark is ready and the wind at help,
Th' associates tend,° and everything is bent   45
For England.

Hamlet.   For England?

King.   Ay, Hamlet.

Hamlet.   Good.

King. So is it, if thou knew'st our purposes.

Hamlet. I see a cherub° that sees them. But come, for
England! Farewell, dear Mother.

King. Thy loving father, Hamlet.   50

Hamlet. My mother—father and mother is man and
wife, man and wife is one flesh, and so, my mother.
Come, for England!   *Exit.*

King. Follow him at foot;° tempt him with speed
aboard.
Delay it not; I'll have him hence tonight.   55
Away! For everything is sealed and done
That else leans° on th' affair. Pray you make haste.
                          [*Exeunt all but the King.*]
And, England, if my love thou hold'st at aught—
As my great power thereof may give thee sense,
Since yet thy cicatrice° looks raw and red   60
After the Danish sword, and thy free awe°
Pays homage to us—thou mayst not coldly set
Our sovereign process,° which imports at full
By letters congruing to that effect
The present° death of Hamlet. Do it, England,   65
For like the hectic° in my blood he rages,
And thou must cure me. Till I know 'tis done,
Howe'er my haps,° my joys were ne'er begun.
                                                        Exit.

---

45 **tend** wait   48 **cherub** angel of knowledge   54 **at foot** closely
57 **leans** depends   60 **cicatrice** scar   61 **free awe** uncompelled sub-
mis-sion   62–63 **coldly set/Our sovereign process** regard slightly
our royal command   65 **present** instant   66 **hectic** fever   68 **haps**
chances, fortunes

[Scene 4. *A plain in Denmark.*]

Enter Fortinbras with his Army over the stage.

Fortinbras. Go, Captain, from me greet the Danish
    king.
    Tell him that by his license Fortinbras
    Craves the conveyance of° a promised march
    Over his kingdom. You know the rendezvous.
5   If that his Majesty would aught with us,
    We shall express our duty in his eye;°
    And let him know so.

Captain.   I will do't, my lord.

Fortinbras. Go softly° on.
                        [*Exeunt all but the Captain.*]
           Enter Hamlet, Rosencrantz, &c.

Hamlet. Good sir, whose powers° are these?

10 *Captain.* They are of Norway, sir.

Hamlet. How purposed, sir, I pray you?

Captain. Against some part of Poland.

Hamlet. Who commands them, sir?

Captain. The nephew to old Norway, Fortinbras.

15 *Hamlet.* Goes it against the main° of Poland, sir,
    Or for some frontier?

Captain. Truly to speak, and with no addition,°
    We go to gain a little patch of ground
    That hath in it no profit but the name.
20   To pay five ducats, five, I would not farm it,
    Nor will it yield to Norway or the Pole
    A ranker° rate, should it be sold in fee.°

4.4.3 **conveyance of** escort for 6 **in his eye** before his eyes (i.e., in his
presence) 8 **softly** slowly 9 **powers** forces 15 **main** main part 17
with no addition plainly 22 **ranker** higher 22 **in fee** out-right

Hamlet. Why, then the Polack never will defend it.

Captain. Yes, it is already garrisoned.

Hamlet. Two thousand souls and twenty thousand
　ducats　　　　　　　　　　　　　　　　　　　25
　Will not debate° the question of this straw.
　This is th' imposthume° of much wealth and peace,
　That inward breaks, and shows no cause without
　Why the man dies. I humbly thank you, sir.

Captain. God bye you, sir.　　　　　　　[*Exit.*]

Rosencrantz.　　　　　Will't please you go, my lord?　30

Hamlet. I'll be with you straight. Go a little before.
　　　　　　　　　　　　[*Exeunt all but Hamlet.*]
　How all occasions do inform against me
　And spur my dull revenge! What is a man,
　If his chief good and market° of his time
　Be but to sleep and feed? A beast, no more.　　35
　Sure he that made us with such large discourse,°
　Looking before and after, gave us not
　That capability and godlike reason
　To fust° in us unused. Now, whether it be
　Bestial oblivion,° or some craven scruple　　40
　Of thinking too precisely on th' event°—
　A thought which, quartered, hath but one part wis-
　　dom
　And ever three parts coward—I do not know
　Why yet I live to say, "This thing's to do,"
　Sith I have cause, and will, and strength, and means　45
　To do't. Examples gross° as earth exhort me.
　Witness this army of such mass and charge,°
　Led by a delicate and tender prince,
　Whose spirit, with divine ambition puffed,
　Makes mouths at the invisible event,°　　50
　Exposing what is mortal and unsure
　To all that fortune, death, and danger dare,

26 **debate** settle　27 **imposthume** abscess, ulcer　34 **market** profit
36 **discourse** understanding　39 **fust** grow moldy　40 **oblivion** forgetfulness　41 **event** outcome　46 **gross** large, obvious　47 **charge** expense　50 **Makes mouths at the invisible event** makes scornful faces
(is contemptuous of) the unseen outcome

Even for an eggshell. Rightly to be great
Is not° to stir without great argument,°
55　But greatly° to find quarrel in a straw
When honor's at the stake. How stand I then,
That have a father killed, a mother stained,
Excitements° of my reason and my blood,
And let all sleep, while to my shame I see
60　The imminent death of twenty thousand men
That for a fantasy and trick of fame°
Go to their graves like beds, fight for a plot
Whereon the numbers cannot try the cause,
Which is not tomb enough and continent°
65　To hide the slain? O, from this time forth,
My thoughts be bloody, or be nothing worth!　　*Exit.*

[Scene 5. *The castle*.]

Enter Horatio, [Queen] Gertrude, and a Gentleman.

Queen. I will not speak with her.

Gentleman. She is importunate, indeed distract.
　Her mood will needs be pitied.

Queen.　　　　　　　　　What would she have?

Gentleman. She speaks much of her father, says she
　　hears
　There's tricks i' th' world, and hems, and beats her
5　　heart,
　Spurns enviously at straws,° speaks things in doubt°
　That carry but half sense. Her speech is nothing,
　Yet the unshapèd use of it doth move

54 **not** (the sense seems to require "not not")　54 **argument** reason
55 **greatly** i.e., nobly　58 **Excitements** incentives　61 **fantasy and
trick of fame** illusion and trifle of reputation　64 **continent** receptacle,
container　4.5.6 **Spurns enviously at straws** objects spitefully to in-
significant matters　6 **in doubt** uncertainly

The hearers to collection;° they yawn° at it,
And botch the words up fit to their own thoughts,   *10*
Which, as her winks and nods and gestures yield
    them,
Indeed would make one think there might be
    thought,
Though nothing sure, yet much unhappily.

Horatio. 'Twere good she were spoken with, for she
    may strew
Dangerous conjectures in ill-breeding minds.   *15*

Queen. Let her come in.   [*Exit Gentleman.*]
[*Aside*] To my sick soul (as sin's true nature is)
Each toy seems prologue to some great amiss;°
So full of artless jealousy° is guilt
It spills° itself in fearing to be spilt.   *20*

> *Enter Ophelia [distracted.]*°

Ophelia. Where is the beauteous majesty of Denmark?

Queen. How now, Ophelia?

Ophelia. (*She sings.*) How should I your truelove know
                From another one?
            By his cockle hat° and staff   *25*
            And his sandal shoon.°

Queen. Alas, sweet lady, what imports this song?

Ophelia. Say you? Nay, pray you mark.
                He is dead and gone, lady,   (*Song*)
                He is dead and gone;   *30*
            At his head a grass-green turf,
            At his heels a stone.
    O, ho!

Queen. Nay, but Ophelia——

Ophelia. Pray you mark.   *35*

8–9 **Yet the . . . to collection** i.e., yet the formless manner of it moves her listeners to gather up some sort of meaning   9 **yawn** gape (?)   18 **amiss** misfortune   19 **artless jealousy** crude suspicion   20 **spills** destroys   20 s.d. the First Quarto says "Enter Ophelia playing on a lute, and her hair down, singing."   25 **cockle hat** (a cockleshell on the hat was the sign of a pilgrim who had journeyed to shrines overseas. The association of lovers and pilgrims was a common one)   26 **shoon** shoes

[*Sings.*] White his shroud as the mountain snow——
               Enter King.

Queen. Alas, look here, my lord.

Ophelia.   Larded° all with sweet flowers (*Song*)
           Which bewept to the grave did not go
40   With truelove showers.

King. How do you, pretty lady?

Ophelia. Well, God dild° you! They say the owl was a
   baker's daughter.° Lord, we know what we are, but
   know not what we may be. God be at your table!

45 *King.* Conceit° upon her father.

Ophelia. Pray let's have no words of this, but when
   they ask you what it means, say you this:
        Tomorrow is Saint Valentine's day.° (*Song*)
          All in the morning betime,
50   And I a maid at your window,
          To be your Valentine.

        Then up he rose and donned his clothes
          And dupped° the chamber door,
        Let in the maid, that out a maid
55   Never departed more.

King. Pretty Ophelia.

Ophelia. Indeed, la, without an oath, I'll make an end
   on't:
   [*Sings.*] By Gis° and by Saint Charity,
        Alack, and fie for shame!
60   Young men will do't if they come to't,
         By Cock,° they are to blame.
        Quoth she, "Before you tumbled me,
         You promised me to wed."

38 **Larded** decorated   42 **dild** yield, i.e., reward   43 **baker's daughter** (an allusion to a tale of a baker's daughter who begrudged bread to Christ and was turned into an owl)   45 **Conceit** brooding   48 **Saint Valentine's day** Feb. 14 (the notion was that a bachelor would become the truelove of the first girl he saw on this day)   53 **dupped** opened (did up)   58 **Gis** (contraction of "Jesus")   61 **Cock** (1) God (2) phallus

He answers:

> "So would I 'a' done, by yonder sun,　　　65
> An thou hadst not come to my bed."

King. How long hath she been thus?

Ophelia. I hope all will be well. We must be patient,
but I cannot choose but weep to think they would
lay him i' th' cold ground. My brother shall know　70
of it; and so I thank you for your good counsel.
Come, my coach! Good night, ladies, good night.
Sweet ladies, good night, good night.　　　　*Exit.*

King. Follow her close; give her good watch, I pray
　　you.　　　　　　　　　　　　　*[Exit Horatio.]*
O, this is the poison of deep grief; it springs　　75
All from her father's death—and now behold!
O Gertrude, Gertrude,
When sorrows come, they come not single spies,
But in battalions: first, her father slain;
Next, your son gone, and he most violent author　80
Of his own just remove; the people muddied,°
Thick and unwholesome in their thoughts and
　　whispers
For good Polonius' death, and we have done but
　　greenly°
In huggermugger° to inter him; poor Ophelia
Divided from herself and her fair judgment,　　85
Without the which we are pictures or mere beasts;
Last, and as much containing as all these,
Her brother is in secret come from France,
Feeds on his wonder,° keeps himself in clouds,
And wants not buzzers° to infect his ear　　　90
With pestilent speeches of his father's death,
Wherein necessity, of matter beggared,°
Will nothing stick° our person to arraign
In ear and ear. O my dear Gertrude, this,

---

81 **muddied** muddled　83 **greenly** foolishly　84 **huggermugger** secret
haste　89 **wonder** suspicion　90 **wants not buzzers** does not lack tale-
bearers　92 **of matter beggared** unprovided with facts　93 **Will nothing stick** will not hesitate

95 Like to a murd'ring piece,° in many places
    Gives me superfluous death.   *A noise within.*

                    Enter a Messenger.

Queen.   Alack, what noise is this?

King. Attend, where are my Switzers?° Let them
    guard the door.
    What is the matter?

Messenger.   Save yourself, my lord.
    The ocean, overpeering of his list,°
100 Eats not the flats with more impiteous haste
    Than young Laertes, in a riotous head,°
    O'erbears your officers. The rabble call him lord,
    And, as the world were now but to begin,
    Antiquity forgot, custom not known,
105 The ratifiers and props of every word,
    They cry, "Choose we! Laertes shall be king!"
    Caps, hands, and tongues applaud it to the clouds,
    "Laertes shall be king! Laertes king!" *A noise within.*

Queen. How cheerfully on the false trail they cry!
110 O, this is counter,° you false Danish dogs!

                Enter Laertes with others.

King. The doors are broke.

Laertes. Where is this king?—Sirs, stand you all
    without.

All. No, let's come in.

Laertes.   I pray you give me leave.

All. We will, we will.

Laertes. I thank you. Keep the door. [*Exeunt his*
115   *Followers.*] O thou vile King,
    Give me my father.

Queen.   Calmly, good Laertes.

---

95 **murd'ring piece** (a cannon that shot a kind of shrapnel) 97
Switzers Swiss guards   99 **list** shore   101 **in a riotous head** with a rebellious force   110 **counter** (a hound runs counter when he follows the
scent backward from the prey)

Laertes. That drop of blood that's calm proclaims me
    bastard,
    Cries cuckold° to my father, brands the harlot
    Even here between the chaste unsmirchèd brow
    Of my true mother.

King.   What is the cause, Laertes,   *120*
    That thy rebellion looks so giantlike?
    Let him go, Gertrude. Do not fear° our person.
    There's such divinity doth hedge a king
    That treason can but peep to° what it would,
    Acts little of his will. Tell me, Laertes,   *125*
    Why thou art thus incensed. Let him go, Gertrude.
    Speak, man.

Laertes. Where is my father?

King.   Dead.

Queen.   But not by him.

King. Let him demand his fill.

Laertes. How came he dead? I'll not be juggled with.   *130*
    To hell allegiance, vows to the blackest devil,
    Conscience and grace to the profoundest pit!
    I dare damnation. To this point I stand,
    That both the worlds I give to negligence,°
    Let come what comes, only I'll be revenged   *135*
    Most throughly for my father.

King.   Who shall stay you?

Laertes. My will, not all the world's.
    And for my means, I'll husband them° so well
    They shall go far with little.

King.   Good Laertes,
    If you desire to know the certainty   *140*
    Of your dear father, is't writ in your revenge
    That swoopstake° you will draw both friend and foe,
    Winner and loser?

---

118 **cuckold** man whose wife is unfaithful   112 **fear** fear for   124
peep to i.e., look at from a distance   134 **That both ... to negligence**
i.e., I care not what may happen (to me) in this world or the next
138 **husband them** use them economically   142 **swoopstake** in a clean
sweep

Laertes. None but his enemies.

King.   Will you know them then?

Laertes. To his good friends thus wide I'll ope my
145   arms
    And like the kind life-rend'ring pelican°
    Repast° them with my blood.

King.   Why, now you speak
    Like a good child and a true gentleman.
    That I am guiltless of your father's death,
150   And am most sensibly° in grief for it,
    It shall as level to your judgment 'pear
    As day does to your eye.
                  A noise within: "Let her come in."

Laertes. How now? What noise is that?

                Enter Ophelia.

    O heat, dry up my brains; tears seven times salt
155   Burn out the sense and virtue° of mine eye!
    By heaven, thy madness shall be paid with weight
    Till our scale turn the beam.° O rose of May,
    Dear maid, kind sister, sweet Ophelia!
    O heavens, is't possible a young maid's wits
160   Should be as mortal as an old man's life?
    Nature is fine° in love, and where 'tis fine,
    It sends some precious instance° of itself
    After the thing it loves.

Ophelia. They bore him barefaced on the bier (*Song*)
165   Hey non nony, nony, hey nony
          And in his grave rained many a tear——
    Fare you well, my dove!

Laertes. Hadst thou thy wits, and didst persuade re-
      venge,
    It could not move thus.

170 *Ophelia.* You must sing "A-down a-down, and you call

---

146 **pelican** (thought to feed its young with its own blood)   147 **Repast**
feed   150 **sensibly** acutely   155 **virtue** power   157 **turn the beam**
weigh down the bar (of the balance)   161 **fine** refined, delicate
162 **instance** sample

him a-down-a." O, how the wheel° becomes it! It is
the false steward, that stole his master's daughter.

Laertes. This nothing's more than matter.°

Ophelia. There's rosemary, that's for remembrance.
Pray you, love, remember. And there is pansies, 175
that's for thoughts.

Laertes. A document° in madness, thoughts and remembrance fitted.

Ophelia. There's fennel° for you, and columbines.
There's rue for you, and here's some for me. We 180
may call it herb of grace o' Sundays. O, you must
wear your rue with a difference. There's a daisy. I
would give you some violets, but they withered all
when my father died. They say 'a made a good end.
[*Sings*]   For bonny sweet Robin is all my joy. 185

Laertes. Thought and affliction, passion, hell itself,
She turns to favor° and to prettiness.

Ophelia.   And will 'a not come again?   (*Song*)
            And will 'a not come again?
                No, no, he is dead,   190
                Go to thy deathbed,
            He never will come again.

            His beard was as white as snow,
            All flaxen was his poll.°
                He is gone, he is gone,   195
                And we cast away moan.
            God 'a' mercy on his soul!
And of all Christian souls, I pray God. God bye you.
                                          [*Exit.*]

---

171 **wheel** (of uncertain meaning, but probably a turn or dance of Ophelia's, rather than Fortune's wheel)   173 **This nothing's more than
matter** this nonsense has more meaning than matters of consequence   177 **document** lesson   179 **fennel** (the distribution of flowers
in the ensuing lines has symbolic meaning, but the meaning is disputed.
Perhaps **fennel,** flattery; **columbines,** cuckoldry; **rue,** sorrow for Ophelia and repentance for the Queen; **daisy,** dissembling; **violets,** faithful-
ness. For other interpretations, see J. W. Lever in *Review of English
Studies,* New Series 3 [1952], pp. 123–29)   187 **favor** charm, beauty
194 **All flaxen was his poll** white as flax was his head

Laertes. Do you see this, O God?

200 *King.* Laertes, I must commune with your grief,
     Or you deny me right. Go but apart,
     Make choice of whom your wisest friends you will,
     And they shall hear and judge 'twixt you and me.
     If by direct or by collateral° hand
205 They find us touched,° we will our kingdom give,
     Our crown, our life, and all that we call ours,
     To you in satisfaction; but if not,
     Be you content to lend your patience to us,
     And we shall jointly labor with your soul
     To give it due content.

210 *Laertes.*   Let this be so.
     His means of death, his obscure funeral—
     No trophy, sword, nor hatchment° o'er his bones,
     No noble rite nor formal ostentation°—
     Cry to be heard, as 'twere from heaven to earth,
     That I must call't in question.

215 *King.*   So you shall;
     And where th' offense is, let the great ax fall.
     I pray you go with me.   *Exeunt.*

[Scene 6. *The castle.*]

Enter Horatio and others.

Horatio. What are they that would speak with me?

Gentleman. Seafaring men, sir. They say they have
     letters for you.

Horatio. Let them come in.   [*Exit Attendant.*]
5   I do not know from what part of the world
     I should be greeted, if not from Lord Hamlet.

---

204 **collateral** indirect   205 **touched** implicated   212 **hatchment** tablet bearing the coat of arms of the dead   213 **ostentation** ceremony

Enter Sailors.

Sailor. God bless you, sir.

Horatio. Let Him bless thee too.

Sailor. 'A shall, sir, an't please Him. There's a letter for you, sir—it came from th' ambassador that was 　　*10* bound for England—if your name be Horatio, as I am let to know it is.

Horatio. [*Reads the letter.*] "Horatio, when thou shalt have overlooked° this, give these fellows some means to the King. They have letters for him. Ere 　*15* we were two days old at sea, a pirate of very warlike appointment° gave us chase. Finding ourselves too slow of sail, we put on a compelled valor, and in the grapple I boarded them. On the instant they got clear of our ship; so I alone became their 　*20* prisoner. They have dealt with me like thieves of mercy, but they knew what they did: I am to do a good turn for them. Let the King have the letters I have sent, and repair thou to me with as much speed as thou wouldest fly death. I have words to 　*25* speak in thine ear will make thee dumb; yet are they much too light for the bore° of the matter. These good fellows will bring thee where I am. Rosencrantz and Guildenstern hold their course for England. Of them I have much to tell thee. Farewell. 　*30*
　　　　　　He that thou knowest thine, HAMLET."
Come, I will give you way for these your letters,
And do't the speedier that you may direct me
To him from whom you brought them. 　　　　*Exeunt.*

4.6.14 **overlooked** surveyed　17 **appointment** equipment　27 **bore** caliber (here, "importance")

[Scene 7. *The castle.*]

Enter King and Laertes.

King. Now must your conscience my acquittance seal,
And you must put me in your heart for friend,
Sith you have heard, and with a knowing ear,
That he which hath your noble father slain
Pursued my life.

5 *Laertes.*   It well appears. But tell me
Why you proceeded not against these feats
So criminal and so capital° in nature,
As by your safety, greatness, wisdom, all things else,
You mainly° were stirred up.

King.   O, for two special reasons,
10 Which may to you perhaps seem much unsinewed,°
But yet to me they're strong. The Queen his mother
Lives almost by his looks, and for myself—
My virtue or my plague, be it either which—
She is so conjunctive° to my life and soul,
15 That, as the star moves not but in his sphere,
I could not but by her. The other motive
Why to a public count° I might not go
Is the great love the general gender° bear him,
Who, dipping all his faults in their affection,
20 Would, like the spring that turneth wood to stone,°
Convert his gyves° to graces; so that my arrows,
Too slightly timbered° for so loud a wind,
Would have reverted to my bow again,
And not where I had aimed them.

4.7.7 **capital** deserving death 9 **mainly** powerfully 10 **unsinewed**
weak 14 **conjunctive** closely united 17 **count** reckoning 18 **general gender** common people 20 **spring that turneth wood to stone** (a
spring in Shakespeare's county was so charged with lime that it would
petrify wood placed in it) 21 **gyves** fetters; G.R. Hibbard's emendation
to *guilts* is attractive 22 **timbered** shafted

Laertes. And so have I a noble father lost, 25
  A sister driven into desp'rate terms,°
  Whose worth, if praises may go back again,°
  Stood challenger on mount of all the age
  For her perfections. But my revenge will come.

King. Break not your sleeps for that. You must not think 30
  That we are made of stuff so flat and dull
  That we can let our beard be shook with danger,
  And think it pastime. You shortly shall hear more.
  I loved your father, and we love ourself,
  And that, I hope, will teach you to imagine—— 35

Enter a Messenger with letters.

  How now? What news?

Messenger. Letters, my lord, from Hamlet:
  These to your Majesty; this to the Queen.

King. From Hamlet? Who brought them?

Messenger. Sailors, my lord, they say; I saw them not. 40
  They were given me by Claudio; he received them
  Of him that brought them.

King. Laertes, you shall hear them.—
  Leave us. *Exit Messenger.*
  [*Reads.*] "High and mighty, you shall know I am set
  naked° on your kingdom. Tomorrow shall I beg
  leave to see your kingly eyes; when I shall (first 45
  asking your pardon thereunto) recount the occasion
  of my sudden and more strange return.
              HAMLET."
  What should this mean? Are all the rest come back?
  Or is it some abuse,° and no such thing? 50

Laertes. Know you the hand?

King. 'Tis Hamlet's character.° "Naked"!

26 **terms** conditions 27 **go back again** revert to what is past 44 **naked** destitute 50 **abuse** deception 51 **character** handwriting

And in a postscript here, he says "alone."
Can you devise° me?

Laertes. I am lost in it, my lord. But let him come.
55   It warms the very sickness in my heart
That I shall live and tell him to his teeth,
"Thus did'st thou."

King.   If it be so, Laertes
(As how should it be so? How otherwise?),
Will you be ruled by me?

Laertes.   Ay, my lord,
60   So you will not o'errule me to a peace.

King. To thine own peace. If he be now returned,
As checking at° his voyage, and that he means
No more to undertake it, I will work him
To an exploit now ripe in my device,
65   Under the which he shall not choose but fall;
And for his death no wind of blame shall breathe,
But even his mother shall uncharge the practice°
And call it accident.

Laertes.   My lord, I will be ruled;
The rather if you could devise it so
That I might be the organ.

70   *King.*   It falls right.
You have been talked of since your travel much,
And that in Hamlet's hearing, for a quality
Wherein they say you shine. Your sum of parts
Did not together pluck such envy from him
75   As did that one, and that, in my regard,
Of the unworthiest siege.°

Laertes.   What part is that, my lord?

King. A very riband in the cap of youth,
Yet needful too, for youth no less becomes
The light and careless livery that it wears
80   Than settled age his sables and his weeds,°
Importing health and graveness. Two months since

---

53 **devise** advise   62 **checking at** turning away from (a term in falconry)   67 **uncharge the practice** not charge the device with treachery
76 **siege** rank   80 **sables and his weeds** i.e., sober attire

Here was a gentleman of Normandy.
I have seen myself, and served against, the French,
And they can° well on horseback, but this gallant
Had witchcraft in't. He grew unto his seat,   *85*
And to such wondrous doing brought his horse
As had he been incorpsed and deminatured
With the brave beast. So far he topped my thought
That I, in forgery° of shapes and tricks,
Come short of what he did.

Laertes.   A Norman was't?   *90*

King. A Norman.

Laertes. Upon my life, Lamord.°

King.   The very same.

Laertes. I know him well. He is the brooch° indeed
   And gem of all the nation.

King. He made confession° of you,   *95*
   And gave you such a masterly report,
   For art and exercise in your defense,
   And for your rapier most especial,
   That he cried out 'twould be a sight indeed
   If one could match you. The scrimers° of their
      nation   *100*
   He swore had neither motion, guard, nor eye,
   If you opposed them. Sir, this report of his
   Did Hamlet so envenom with his envy
   That he could nothing do but wish and beg
   Your sudden coming o'er to play with you.   *105*
   Now, out of this——

Laertes.   What out of this, my lord?

King. Laertes, was your father dear to you?
   Or are you like the painting of a sorrow,
   A face without a heart?

Laertes.   Why ask you this?

King. Not that I think you did not love your father,   *110*

84 **can** do   89 **forgery** invention   92 **Lamord** (the name suggests *la mort,* i.e. death [French])   93 **brooch** ornament   95 **confession** report 100 **scrimers** fencers

But that I know love is begun by time,
And that I see, in passages of proof,°
Time qualifies° the spark and fire of it.
There lives within the very flame of love
115   A kind of wick or snuff° that will abate it,
And nothing is at a like goodness still,°
For goodness, growing to a plurisy,°
Dies in his own too-much. That we would do
We should do when we would, for this "would"
    changes,
120   And hath abatements and delays as many
As there are tongues, are hands, are accidents,
And then this "should" is like a spendthrift sigh,°
That hurts by easing. But to the quick° of th' ulcer—
Hamlet comes back; what would you undertake
125   To show yourself in deed your father's son
More than in words?

Laertes.   To cut his throat i' th' church!

King. No place indeed should murder sanctuarize;°
Revenge should have no bounds. But, good Laertes,
Will you do this? Keep close within your chamber.
130   Hamlet returned shall know you are come home.
We'll put on those° shall praise your excellence
And set a double varnish on the fame
The Frenchman gave you, bring you in fine°
    together
And wager on your heads. He, being remiss,
135   Most generous, and free from all contriving,
Will not peruse the foils, so that with ease,
Or with a little shuffling, you may choose
A sword unbated,° and, in a pass of practice,°
Requite him for your father.

Laertes.   I will do't,

112 **passages of proof** proved cases   113 **qualifies** diminishes   115 **snuff** residue of burnt wick (which dims the light)   116 **still** always   117 **plurisy** fullness, excess   122 **spendthrift sigh** (sighing provides ease, but because it was thought to thin the blood and so shorten life it was spendthrift)   123 **quick** sensitive flesh   127 **sanctuarize** protect   131 **We'll put on those** we'll incite persons who   133 **in fine** finally   138 **unbated** not blunted   138 **pass of practice** treacherous thrust

And for that purpose I'll anoint my sword.   *140*
I bought an unction of a mountebank,°
So mortal that, but dip a knife in it,
Where it draws blood, no cataplasm° so rare,
Collected from all simples° that have virtue°
Under the moon, can save the thing from death   *145*
That is but scratched withal. I'll touch my point
With this contagion, that, if I gall him slightly,
It may be death.

King.   Let's further think of this,
Weigh what convenience both of time and means
May fit us to our shape.° If this should fail,   *150*
And that our drift look through° our bad per-
    formance,
'Twere better not assayed. Therefore this project
Should have a back or second, that might hold
If this did blast in proof.° Soft, let me see.
We'll make a solemn wager on your cunnings—   *155*
I ha't!
When in your motion you are hot and dry—
As make your bouts more violent to that end—
And that he calls for drink, I'll have prepared him
A chalice for the nonce,° whereon but sipping,   *160*
If he by chance escape your venomed stuck,°
Our purpose may hold there.—But stay, what noise?

                    Enter Queen.

Queen. One woe doth tread upon another's heel.
So fast they follow. Your sister's drowned, Laertes.

Laertes. Drowned! O, where?   *165*

Queen. There is a willow grows askant° the brook,
That shows his hoar° leaves in the glassy stream:
Therewith° fantastic garlands did she make
Of crowflowers, nettles, daisies, and long purples,

---

141 **mountebank** quack   143 **cataplasm** poultice   144 **simples** medici-
nal herbs   144 **virtue** power (to heal)   150 **shape** role   151 **drift look
through** purpose show through   154 **blast in proof** burst (fail) in per-
formance   160 **nonce** occasion   161 **stuck** thrust   166 **askant** aslant
167 **hoar** silver-gray   168 **Therewith** i.e., with willow twigs

170 That liberal° shepherds give a grosser name,
But our cold maids do dead men's fingers call them.
There on the pendent boughs her crownet° weeds
Clamb'ring to hang, an envious sliver° broke,
When down her weedy trophies and herself
175 Fell in the weeping brook. Her clothes spread wide,
And mermaidlike awhile they bore her up,
Which time she chanted snatches of old lauds,°
As one incapable° of her own distress,
Or like a creature native and indued°
180 Unto that element. But long it could not be
Till that her garments, heavy with their drink,
Pulled the poor wretch from her melodious lay
To muddy death.

Laertes.   Alas, then she is drowned?

Queen. Drowned, drowned.

185 Laertes. Too much of water hast thou, poor Ophelia,
And therefore I forbid my tears; but yet
It is our trick;° nature her custom holds,
Let shame say what it will: when these° are gone,
The woman° will be out. Adieu, my lord.
190 I have a speech o' fire, that fain would blaze,
But that this folly drowns it.   *Exit.*

King.   Let's follow, Gertrude.
How much I had to do to calm his rage!
Now fear I this will give it start again;
Therefore let's follow.   *Exeunt.*

---

170 **liberal** free-spoken, coarse-mouthed   172 **crownet** coronet   173
envious sliver malicious branch   177 **lauds** hymns   178 **incapable** un-
aware   179 **indued** in harmony with   187 **trick** trait, way   188 **these**
the tears he is shedding   189 **woman** i.e., womanly part of me

[ACT 5

Scene 1. *A churchyard.*]

Enter two Clowns.°

Clown. Is she to be buried in Christian burial when she willfully seeks her own salvation?

Other. I tell thee she is. Therefore make her grave straight.° The crowner° hath sate on her, and finds it Christian burial. 5

Clown. How can that be, unless she drowned herself in her own defense?

Other. Why, 'tis found so.

Clown. It must be *se offendendo*;° it cannot be else. For here lies the point: if I drown myself wittingly, 10 it argues an act, and an act hath three branches— it is to act, to do, to perform. Argal,° she drowned herself wittingly.

Other. Nay, but hear you, Goodman Delver.

Clown. Give me leave. Here lies the water—good. 15 Here stands the man—good. If the man go to this water and drown himself, it is, will he nill he,° he goes; mark you that. But if the water come to him and drown him, he drowns not himself. Argal, he

---

5.1.s.d. **Clowns** rustics (the first clown is a grave-digger) 4 **straight** straightway 4 **crowner** coroner 9 **se offendendo** (blunder for *se defendendo*, a legal term meaning "in self-defense") 12 **Argal** (blunder for Latin *ergo*, "therefore") 17 **will he nill he** will he or will he not (whether he will or will not)

20 that is not guilty of his own death, shortens not his
    own life.

Other. But is this law?

Clown. Ay marry, is't—crowner's quest° law.

Other. Will you ha' the truth on't? If this had not been
25 a gentlewoman, she should have been buried out
    o' Christian burial.

Clown. Why, there thou say'st. And the more pity
    that great folk should have count'nance° in this
    world to drown or hang themselves more than their
30 even-Christen.° Come, my spade. There is no an-
    cient gentlemen but gard'ners, ditchers, and grave-
    makers. They hold up° Adam's profession.

Other. Was he a gentleman?

Clown. 'A was the first that ever bore arms.°

35 *Other.* Why, he had none.

Clown. What, art a heathen? How dost thou under-
    stand the Scripture? The Scripture says Adam
    digged. Could he dig without arms? I'll put another
    question to thee. If thou answerest me not to the
40 purpose, confess thyself——

Other. Go to.

Clown. What is he that builds stronger than either the
    mason, the shipwright, or the carpenter?

Other. The gallowsmaker, for that frame outlives a
45 thousand tenants.

Clown. I like thy wit well, in good faith. The gallows
    does well. But how does it well? It does well to those
    that do ill. Now thou dost ill to say the gallows
    is built stronger than the church. Argal, the gallows
50 may do well to thee. To't again, come.

Other. Who builds stronger than a mason, a ship-
    wright, or a carpenter?

---

23 **quest** inquest   28 **count'nance** privilege   30 **even-Christen** fellow
Christian   32 **hold up** keep up   34 **bore arms** had a coat of arms (the
sign of a gentleman)

Clown. Ay, tell me that, and unyoke.°

Other. Marry, now I can tell.

Clown. To't.   55

Other. Mass,° I cannot tell.

Enter Hamlet and Horatio afar off.

Clown. Cudgel thy brains no more about it, for your
dull ass will not mend his pace with beating. And
when you are asked this question next, say "a grave-
maker." The houses he makes lasts till doomsday.   60
Go, get thee in, and fetch me a stoup° of liquor.
                                         [*Exit Other Clown.*]

In youth when I did love, did love,   (*Song*)
     Methought it was very sweet
To contract—O—the time for—a—my behove,°
     O, methought there—a—was nothing—a—meet.   65

Hamlet. Has this fellow no feeling of his business? 'A
sings in gravemaking.

Horatio. Custom hath made it in him a property of
easiness.°

Hamlet. 'Tis e'en so. The hand of little employment   70
hath the daintier sense.°

Clown.   But age with his stealing steps   (*Song*)
          Hath clawed me in his clutch,
       And hath shipped me into the land,
          As if I had never been such.   75
                                         [*Throws up a skull.*]

Hamlet. That skull had a tongue in it, and could sing
once. How the knave jowls° it to the ground, as if
'twere Cain's jawbone, that did the first murder!
This might be the pate of a politician, which this

---

53 **unyoke** i.e., stop work for the day   56 **Mass** by the mass   61 **stoup**
tankard   64 **behove** advantage   68–69 **in him a property of easiness**
easy for him   71 **hath the daintier sense** is more sensitive (because it
is not calloused)   77 **jowls** hurls

80   ass now o'erreaches,° one that would circumvent
      God, might it not?

Horatio. It might, my lord.

Hamlet. Or of a courtier, which could say "Good
      morrow, sweet lord! How dost thou, sweet lord?"
85   This might be my Lord Such-a-one, that praised
      my Lord Such-a-one's horse when 'a went to beg
      it, might it not?

Horatio. Ay, my lord.

Hamlet. Why, e'en so, and now my Lady Worm's,
90   chapless,° and knocked about the mazzard° with a
      sexton's spade. Here's fine revolution, an we had
      the trick to see't. Did these bones cost no more
      the breeding but to play at loggets° with them?
      Mine ache to think on't.

95 *Clown.*   A pickax and a spade, a spade,   (*Song*)
                 For and a shrouding sheet;
              O, a pit of clay for to be made
                 For such a guest is meet.

                                    [*Throws up another skull.*]

Hamlet. There's another. Why may not that be the
100   skull of a lawyer? Where be his quiddities° now, his
      quillities,° his cases, his tenures,° and his tricks?
      Why does he suffer this mad knave now to knock
      him about the sconce° with a dirty shovel, and will
      not tell him of his action of battery? Hum! This
105   fellow might be in's time a great buyer of land, with
      his statutes, his recognizances, his fines,° his double
      vouchers, his recoveries. Is this the fine° of his fines,
      and the recovery of his recoveries, to have his fine
      pate full of fine dirt? Will his vouchers vouch him

---

80 **o'erreaches** (1) reaches over (2) has the advantage over   90 **chapless** lacking the lower jaw   90 **mazzard** head   93 **loggets** (a game in
which small pieces of wood were thrown at an object)   100 **quiddities**
subtle arguments (from Latin *quidditas,* "whatness")   101 **quillities**
fine distinctions   101 **tenures** legal means of holding land   103 **sconce**
head   106 **his statutes, his recognizances, his fines** his documents
giving a creditor control of a debtor's land, his bonds of surety, his documents changing an entailed estate into fee simple (unrestricted owner-
ship)   107 **fine** end

no more of his purchases, and double ones too, than   *110*
the length and breadth of a pair of indentures?°
The very conveyances° of his lands will scarcely
lie in this box, and must th' inheritor himself have no
more, ha?

Horatio. Not a jot more, my lord.   *115*

Hamlet. Is not parchment made of sheepskins?

Horatio. Ay, my lord, and of calveskins too.

Hamlet. They are sheep and calves which seek out
assurance° in that. I will speak to this fellow. Whose
grave's this, sirrah?   *120*

Clown. Mine, sir.
[*Sings.*]   O, a pit of clay for to be made
                 For such a guest is meet.

Hamlet. I think it be thine indeed, for thou liest in't.

Clown. You lie out on't, sir, and therefore 'tis not   *125*
yours. For my part, I do not lie in't, yet it is mine.

Hamlet. Thou dost lie in't, to be in't and say it is
thine. 'Tis for the dead, not for the quick;° therefore thou liest.

Clown. 'Tis a quick lie, sir; 'twill away again from   *130*
me to you.

Hamlet. What man dost thou dig it for?

Clown. For no man, sir.

Hamlet. What woman then?

Clown. For none neither.   *135*

Hamlet. Who is to be buried in't?

Clown. One that was a woman, sir; but, rest her soul,
she's dead.

Hamlet. How absolute° the knave is! We must speak by
the card,° or equivocation° will undo us. By the   *140*

---

111 **indentures** contracts   112 **conveyances** legal documents for the
transference of land   119 **assurance** safety   128 **quick** living
139 **absolute** positive, decided   139–40 **by the card** by the compass
card, i.e., exactly   140 **equivocation** ambiguity

Lord, Horatio, this three years I have took note of
it, the age is grown so picked° that the toe of the
peasant comes so near the heel of the courtier he
galls his kibe.° How long hast thou been a grave-
145 maker?

Clown. Of all the days i' th' year, I came to't that day
that our last king Hamlet overcame Fortinbras.

Hamlet. How long is that since?

Clown. Cannot you tell that? Every fool can tell that. It
150 was that very day that young Hamlet was born—
he that is mad, and sent into England.

Hamlet. Ay, marry, why was he sent into England?

Clown. Why, because 'a was mad. 'A shall recover his
wits there; or, if 'a do not, 'tis no great matter there.

155 *Hamlet.* Why?

Clown. 'Twill not be seen in him there. There the men
are as mad as he.

Hamlet. How came he mad?

Clown. Very strangely, they say.

160 *Hamlet.* How strangely?

Clown. Faith, e'en with losing his wits.

Hamlet. Upon what ground?

Clown. Why, here in Denmark. I have been sexton
here, man and boy, thirty years.

165 *Hamlet.* How long will a man lie i' th' earth ere he rot?

Clown. Faith, if 'a be not rotten before 'a die (as we
have many pocky corses° nowadays that will scarce
hold the laying in), 'a will last you some eight year
or nine year. A tanner will last you nine year.

170 *Hamlet.* Why he, more than another?

Clown. Why, sir, his hide is so tanned with his trade

142 **picked** refined   144 **kibe** sore on the back of the heel   167 **pocky
corses** bodies of persons who had been infected with the pox (syphilis)

that 'a will keep out water a great while, and your water is a sore decayer of your whoreson dead body. Here's a skull now hath lien you i' th' earth three and twenty years.   *175*

Hamlet. Whose was it?

Clown. A whoreson mad fellow's it was. Whose do you think it was?

Hamlet. Nay, I know not.

Clown. A pestilence on him for a mad rogue! 'A poured   *180* a flagon of Rhenish on my head once. This same skull, sir, was, sir, Yorick's skull, the King's jester.

Hamlet. This?

Clown. E'en that.

Hamlet. Let me see. [*Takes the skull.*] Alas, poor   *185* Yorick! I knew him, Horatio, a fellow of infinite jest, of most excellent fancy. He hath borne me on his back a thousand times. And now how abhorred in my imagination it is! My gorge rises at it. Here hung those lips that I have kissed I know not how   *190* oft. Where be your gibes now? Your gambols, your songs, your flashes of merriment that were wont to set the table on a roar? Not one now to mock your own grinning? Quite chapfall'n°? Now get you to my lady's chamber, and tell her, let her paint an inch   *195* thick, to this favor° she must come. Make her laugh at that. Prithee, Horatio, tell me one thing.

Horatio. What's that, my lord?

Hamlet. Dost thou think Alexander looked o' this fashion i' th' earth?   *200*

Horatio. E'en so.

Hamlet. And smelt so? Pah!   [*Puts down the skull.*]

Horatio. E'en so, my lord.

---

194 **chapfall'n** (1) down in the mouth (2) jawless   196 **favor** facial appearance

Hamlet. To what base uses we may return, Horatio!
205   Why may not imagination trace the noble dust of
Alexander till 'a find it stopping a bunghole?

Horatio. 'Twere to consider too curiously,° to consider
so.

Hamlet. No, faith, not a jot, but to follow him thither
210   with modesty enough,° and likelihood to lead it; as
thus: Alexander died, Alexander was buried, Alexander returneth to dust; the dust is earth; of earth
we make loam; and why of that loam whereto he was
converted might they not stop a beer barrel?
215   Imperious Caesar, dead and turned to clay,
Might stop a hole to keep the wind away.
O, that that earth which kept the world in awe
Should patch a wall t' expel the winter's flaw!°
But soft, but soft awhile! Here comes the King.

Enter King, Queen, Laertes, and a coffin, with Lords
attendant [*and a Doctor of Divinity*].

220   The Queen, the courtiers. Who is this they follow?
And with such maimèd° rites? This doth betoken
The corse they follow did with desp'rate hand
Fordo it° own life. 'Twas of some estate.°
Couch° we awhile, and mark. [*Retires with Horatio.*]

Laertes. What ceremony else?

225 *Hamlet.*   That is Laertes,
A very noble youth. Mark.

Laertes. What ceremony else?

Doctor. Her obsequies have been as far enlarged
As we have warranty. Her death was doubtful,°
230   And, but that great command o'ersways the order,
She should in ground unsanctified been lodged
Till the last trumpet. For charitable prayers,

---

207 **curiously** minutely   210 **with modesty enough** without exaggera-
tion   218 **flaw** gust   221 **maimèd** incomplete   223 **Fordo it** destroy
its   223 **estate** high rank   224 **Couch** hide   229 **doubtful** suspicious

Shards,° flints, and pebbles should be thrown on her.
Yet here she is allowed her virgin crants,°
Her maiden strewments,° and the bringing home   235
Of bell and burial.

Laertes. Must there no more be done?

Doctor.   No more be done.
We should profane the service of the dead
To sing a requiem and such rest to her
As to peace-parted souls.

Laertes.   ⸜ Lay her i' th' earth,   240
And from her fair and unpolluted flesh
May violets spring! I tell thee, churlish priest,
A minist'ring angel shall my sister be
When thou liest howling!

Hamlet.   What, the fair Ophelia?

Queen. Sweets to the sweet! Farewell.   245
                    [*Scatters flowers.*]
I hoped thou shouldst have been my Hamlet's wife.
I thought thy bride bed to have decked, sweet maid,
And not have strewed thy grave.

Laertes.   O, treble woe
Fall ten times treble on that cursèd head
Whose wicked deed thy most ingenious sense°   250
Deprived thee of! Hold off the earth awhile,
Till I have caught her once more in mine arms.
                    Leaps in the grave.
Now pile your dust upon the quick and dead
Till of this flat a mountain you have made
T'o'ertop old Pelion° or the skyish head   255
Of blue Olympus.

Hamlet.   [*Coming forward*] What is he whose grief

---

233 **Shards** broken pieces of pottery   234 **crants** garlands   235 **strewments** i.e., of flowers   250 **most ingenious sense** finely endowed mind
255 **Pelion** (according to classical legend, giants in their fight with the gods sought to reach heaven by piling Mount Pelion and Mount Ossa on Mount Olympus)

Bears such an emphasis, whose phrase of sorrow
Conjures the wand'ring stars,° and makes them
    stand
Like wonder-wounded hearers? This is I,
Hamlet the Dane.

260 *Laertes.*   The devil take thy soul!
                        [*Grapples with him.*]°

Hamlet. Thou pray'st not well.
I prithee take thy fingers from my throat,
For, though I am not splenitive° and rash,
Yet have I in me something dangerous,
265 Which let thy wisdom fear. Hold off thy hand.

King. Pluck them asunder.

Queen.   Hamlet, Hamlet!

All. Gentlemen!

Horatio.   Good my lord, be quiet.
                        [*Attendants part them.*]

Hamlet. Why, I will fight with him upon this theme
Until my eyelids will no longer wag.

270 *Queen.* O my son, what theme?

Hamlet. I loved Ophelia. Forty thousand brothers
Could not with all their quantity of love
Make up my sum. What wilt thou do for her?

King. O, he is mad, Laertes.

275 *Queen.* For love of God forbear him.

Hamlet. 'Swounds, show me what thou't do.
Woo't weep? Woo't fight? Woo't fast? Woo't tear
    thyself?
Woo't drink up eisel?° Eat a crocodile?

258 **wand'ring stars** planets   260 s.d. **Grapples with him** (Q1, a bad quarto, presumably reporting a version that toured, has a previous direction saying "Hamlet leaps in after Laertes." Possibly he does so, somewhat hysterically. But such a direction—absent from the two good texts, Q2 and F—makes Hamlet the aggressor, somewhat contradicting his next speech. Perhaps Laertes leaps out of the grave to attack Hamlet)   263 **splenitive** fiery (the spleen was thought to be the seat of anger)   278 **eisel** vinegar

I'll do't. Dost thou come here to whine?
To outface me with leaping in her grave?   280
Be buried quick with her, and so will I.
And if thou prate of mountains, let them throw
Millions of acres on us, till our ground,
Singeing his pate against the burning zone,°
Make Ossa like a wart! Nay, an thou'lt mouth,   285
I'll rant as well as thou.

Queen.   This is mere madness;
And thus a while the fit will work on him.
Anon, as patient as the female dove
When that her golden couplets are disclosed,°
His silence will sit drooping.

Hamlet.   Hear you, sir.   290
What is the reason that you use me thus?
I loved you ever. But it is no matter.
Let Hercules himself do what he may,
The cat will mew, and dog will have his day.

King. I pray thee, good Horatio, wait upon him.   295
                    Exit Hamlet and Horatio.
[*To Laertes*] Strengthen your patience in our last
    night's speech.
We'll put the matter to the present push.°
Good Gertrude, set some watch over your son.
This grave shall have a living° monument.
An hour of quiet shortly shall we see;   300
Till then in patience our proceeding be.   *Exeunt.*

---

284 **burning zone** sun's orbit   289 **golden couplets are disclosed** (the
dove lays two eggs, and the newly hatched [**disclosed**] young are cov-
ered with golden down)   297 **present push** immediate test   299 **living**
lasting (with perhaps also a reference to the plot against Hamlet's life)

[Scene 2. *The castle.*]

Enter Hamlet and Horatio.

Hamlet. So much for this, sir; now shall you see the
    other.
    You do remember all the circumstance?

Horatio. Remember it, my lord!

Hamlet. Sir, in my heart there was a kind of fighting
5   That would not let me sleep. Methought I lay
    Worse than the mutines in the bilboes.° Rashly
    (And praised be rashness for it) let us know,
    Our indiscretion sometime serves us well
    When our deep plots do pall,° and that should learn
    us
10   There's a divinity that shapes our ends,
    Rough-hew them how we will.

Horatio.   That is most certain.

Hamlet. Up from my cabin,
    My sea gown scarfed about me, in the dark
    Groped I to find out them, had my desire,
15   Fingered° their packet, and in fine° withdrew
    To mine own room again, making so bold,
    My fears forgetting manners, to unseal
    Their grand commission; where I found, Horatio—
    Ah, royal knavery!—an exact command,
20   Larded° with many several sorts of reasons,
    Importing Denmark's health, and England's too,
    With, ho, such bugs and goblins in my life,°
    That on the supervise,° no leisure bated,°
    No, not to stay the grinding of the ax,

5.2.6 **mutines in the bilboes** mutineers in fetters   9 **pall** fail   15 **Fingered** stole   15 **in fine** finally   20 **Larded** enriched   22 **such bugs and goblins in my life** such bugbears and imagined terrors if I were allowed to live   23 **supervise** reading   23 **leisure bated** delay allowed

My head should be struck off.

Horatio.   Is't possible?   25

Hamlet. Here's the commission; read it at more leisure.
But wilt thou hear now how I did proceed?

Horatio. I beseech you.

Hamlet. Being thus benetted round with villains,
Or° I could make a prologue to my brains,   30
They had begun the play. I sat me down,
Devised a new commission, wrote it fair.
I once did hold it, as our statists° do,
A baseness to write fair,° and labored much
How to forget that learning, but, sir, now   35
It did me yeoman's service. Wilt thou know
Th' effect° of what I wrote?

Horatio.   Ay, good my lord.

Hamlet. An earnest conjuration from the King,
As England was his faithful tributary,
As love between them like the palm might flourish,   40
As peace should still her wheaten garland wear
And stand a comma° 'tween their amities,
And many suchlike as's of great charge,°
That on the view and knowing of these contents,
Without debatement further, more or less,   45
He should those bearers put to sudden death,
Not shriving° time allowed.

Horatio.   How was this sealed?

Hamlet. Why, even in that was heaven ordinant.°
I had my father's signet in my purse,
Which was the model° of that Danish seal,   50
Folded the writ up in the form of th' other,
Subscribed it, gave't th' impression, placed it safely,
The changeling never known. Now, the next day
Was our sea fight, and what to this was sequent
Thou knowest already.   55

---

30 **Or** ere   33 **statists** statesmen   34 **fair** clearly   37 **effect** purport
42 **comma** link   43 **great charge** (1) serious exhortation (2) heavy burden (punning on *as's* and "asses")   47 **shriving** absolution   48 **ordinant** ruling   50 **model** counterpart

Horatio. So Guildenstern and Rosencrantz go to't.

Hamlet. Why, man, they did make love to this employ-
     ment.
     They are not near my conscience; their defeat
     Does by their own insinuation° grow.
60   'Tis dangerous when the baser nature comes
     Between the pass° and fell incensèd points°
     Of mighty opposites.

Horatio.   Why, what a king is this!

Hamlet. Does it not, think thee, stand me now upon°—
     He that hath killed my king, and whored my mother,
65   Popped in between th' election° and my hopes,
     Thrown out his angle° for my proper life,°
     And with such coz'nage°—is't not perfect con-
     science
     To quit° him with this arm? And is't not to be
     damned
     To let this canker of our nature come
70   In further evil?

Horatio. It must be shortly known to him from England
     What is the issue of the business there.

Hamlet. It will be short; the interim's mine,
     And a man's life's no more than to say "one."
75   But I am very sorry, good Horatio,
     That to Laertes I forgot myself,
     For by the image of my cause I see
     The portraiture of his. I'll court his favors.
     But sure the bravery° of his grief did put me
     Into a tow'ring passion.

80 *Horatio.*   Peace, who comes here?

          Enter young Osric, a courtier.

Osric. Your lordship is right welcome back to Den-
     mark.

59 **insinuation** meddling 61 **pass** thrust 61 **fell incensèd points**
fiercely angry rapiers 63 **stand me now upon** become incumbent upon
me 65 **election** (the Danish monarchy was elective) 66 **angle** fishing
line 66 **my proper life** my own life 67 **coz'nage** trickery (and with a
pun on *cousinage,* kinship) 68 **quit** pay back 79 **bravery** bravado

Hamlet. I humbly thank you, sir. [*Aside to Horatio*] Dost know this waterfly?°

Horatio. [*Aside to Hamlet*] No, my good lord.

Hamlet. [*Aside to Horatio*] Thy state is the more gra-   85
cious, for 'tis a vice to know him. He hath much
land, and fertile. Let a beast be lord of beasts, and
his crib shall stand at the king's mess.° 'Tis a
chough,° but, as I say, spacious° in the possession
of dirt.   90

Osric. Sweet lord, if your lordship were at leisure, I
should impart a thing to you from his Majesty.

Hamlet. I will receive it, sir, with all diligence of spirit.
Put your bonnet to his right use. 'Tis for the head.

Osric. I thank your lordship, it is very hot.   95

Hamlet. No, believe me, 'tis very cold; the wind is
northerly.

Osric. It is indifferent cold, my lord, indeed.

Hamlet. But yet methinks it is very sultry and hot for
my complexion.°   100

Osric. Exceedingly, my lord; it is very sultry, as 'twere—
I cannot tell how. But, my lord, his Majesty bade
me signify to you that 'a has laid a great wager on
your head. Sir, this is the matter——

Hamlet. I beseech you remember.   105
[*Hamlet moves him to put on his hat.*]

Osric. Nay, good my lord; for my ease, in good faith.
Sir, here is newly come to court Laertes—believe
me, an absolute gentleman, full of most excellent
differences,° of very soft society and great showing.
Indeed, to speak feelingly° of him, he is the card°   110
or calendar of gentry; for you shall find in him the
continent° of what part a gentleman would see.

---

83 **waterfly** (Osric's costume—perhaps a hat with plumes—suggests an insect's wings) · 88 **mess** table   89 **chough** jackdaw (here, chatterer) 89 **spacious** well off   100 **complexion** temperament   109 **differences** distinguishing characteristics   110 **feelingly** justly   110 **card** chart 112 **continent** summary

Hamlet. Sir, his definement° suffers no perdition° in
you, though, I know, to divide him inventorially
115 would dozy° th' arithmetic of memory, and yet but
yaw neither in respect of his quick sail.° But, in the
verity of extolment, I take him to be a soul of great
article,° and his infusion° of such dearth and rare-
ness as, to make true diction° of him, his semblable°
120 is his mirror, and who else would trace him, his um-
brage,° nothing more.

Osric. Your lordship speaks most infallibly of him.

Hamlet. The concernancy,° sir? Why do we wrap the
gentleman in our more rawer breath?

125 *Osric.* Sir?

Horatio. Is't not possible to understand in another
tongue? You will to't,° sir, really.

Hamlet. What imports the nomination of this gentleman?

130 *Osric.* Of Laertes?

Horatio. [*Aside to Hamlet*] His purse is empty already.
All's golden words are spent.

Hamlet. Of him, sir.

Osric. I know you are not ignorant——

135 *Hamlet.* I would you did, sir; yet, in faith, if you did, it
would not much approve° me. Well, sir?

Osric. You are not ignorant of what excellence Laertes
is——

Hamlet. I dare not confess that, lest I should compare
140 with him in excellence; but to know a man well were
to know himself.

---

113 **definement** description 113 **perdition** loss 115 **dozy** dizzy
115–16 **and yet . . . quick sail** i.e., and yet only stagger despite all (**yaw
neither**) in trying to overtake his virtues 118 **article** (literally, "item,"
but here perhaps "traits" or "importance") 118 **infusion** essential quality 119 **diction** description 119 **semblable** likeness 120–21 **um-
brage** shadow 123 **concernancy** meaning 127 **will to't** will get there
136 **approve** commend

Osric. I mean, sir, for his weapon; but in the imputa-
tion° laid on him by them, in his meed° he's un-
fellowed.

Hamlet. What's his weapon?   *145*

Osric. Rapier and dagger.

Hamlet. That's two of his weapons—but well.

Osric. The King, sir, hath wagered with him six Bar-
bary horses, against the which he has impawned,° as
I take it, six French rapiers and poniards, with their   *150*
assigns,° as girdle, hangers,° and so. Three of the
carriages,° in faith, are very dear to fancy, very re-
sponsive° to the hilts, most delicate carriages, and
of very liberal conceit.°

Hamlet. What call you the carriages?   *155*

Horatio. [*Aside to Hamlet*] I knew you must be edified
by the margent° ere you had done.

Osric. The carriages, sir, are the hangers.

Hamlet. The phrase would be more germane to the
matter if we could carry a cannon by our sides. I   *160*
would it might be hangers till then. But on! Six Bar-
bary horses against six French swords, their assigns,
and three liberal-conceited carriages—that's the
French bet against the Danish. Why is this all im-
pawned, as you call it?   *165*

Osric. The King, sir, hath laid, sir, that in a dozen
passes between yourself and him he shall not exceed
you three hits; he hath laid on twelve for nine, and
it would come to immediate trial if your lordship
would vouchsafe the answer.   *170*

Hamlet. How if I answer no?

Osric. I mean, my lord, the opposition of your person
in trial.

142–43 **imputation** reputation   143 **meed** merit   149 **impawned** wagered   151 **assigns** accompaniments   151 **hangers** straps hanging the
sword to the belt   152 **carriages** (an affected word for hangers)
152–53 **responsive** corresponding   154 **liberal conceit** elaborate de-
sign   57 **margent** i.e., marginal (explanatory) comment

Hamlet. Sir, I will walk here in the hall. If it please
175 his Majesty, it is the breathing time of day with me.°
Let the foils be brought, the gentleman willing, and
the King hold his purpose, I will win for him an I
can; if not, I will gain nothing but my shame and
the odd hits.

180 *Osric.* Shall I deliver you e'en so?

Hamlet. To this effect, sir, after what flourish your
nature will.

Osric. I commend my duty to your lordship.

Hamlet. Yours, yours. [*Exit Osric.*] He does well to
185 commend it himself; there are no tongues else for's
turn.

Horatio. This lapwing° runs away with the shell on his
head.

Hamlet. 'A did comply, sir, with his dug° before 'a
190 sucked it. Thus has he, and many more of the
same breed that I know the drossy age dotes on,
only got the tune of the time and, out of an habit of
encounter,° a kind of yeasty° collection, which
carries them through and through the most fanned
195 and winnowed opinions; and do but blow them to
their trial, the bubbles are out.°

Enter a Lord.

Lord. My lord, his Majesty commended him to you by
young Osric, who brings back to him that you
attend him in the hall. He sends to know if your
200 pleasure hold to play with Laertes, or that you will
take longer time.

Hamlet. I am constant to my purposes; they follow the

---

175 **breathing time of day with me** time when I take exercise   187 **lapwing** (the new-hatched lapwing was thought to run around
with half its shell on its head)   189 **'A did comply, sir, with his dug** he
was ceremoniously polite to his mother's breast   192–93 **out of an
habit of encounter** out of his own superficial way of meeting and con-
versing with people   193 **yeasty** frothy   196 **the bubbles are out** i.e.,
they are blown away (the reference is to the "yeasty collection")

King's pleasure. If his fitness speaks, mine is ready;
now or whensoever, provided I be so able as now.

Lord. The King and Queen and all are coming down.   205

Hamlet. In happy time.°

Lord. The Queen desires you to use some gentle enter-
tainment° to Laertes before you fall to play.

Hamlet. She well instructs me.   [*Exit Lord.*]

Horatio. You will lose this wager, my lord.   210

Hamlet. I do not think so. Since he went into France
I have been in continual practice. I shall win at the
odds. But thou wouldst not think how ill all's here
about my heart. But it is no matter.

Horatio. Nay, good my lord——   215

Hamlet. It is but foolery, but it is such a kind of gain-
giving° as would perhaps trouble a woman.

Horatio. If your mind dislike anything, obey it. I will
forestall their repair hither and say you are not fit.

Hamlet. Not a whit, we defy augury. There is special   220
providence in the fall of a sparrow.° If it be now,
'tis not to come; if it be not to come, it will be now;
if it be not now, yet it will come. The readiness is
all. Since no man of aught he leaves knows, what
is't to leave betimes?° Let be.   225

*A table prepared. [Enter] Trumpets, Drums, and
Officers with cushions; King, Queen, [Osric,] and
all the State, [with] foils, daggers, [and stoups
of wine borne in]; and Laertes.*

King. Come, Hamlet, come, and take this hand from
me.

          [*The King puts Laertes' hand into Hamlet's.*]

---

206 **In happy time** It is an opportune time   207–08 **to use some gentle
entertainment** to be courteous   217 **gaingiving** misgiving   221 **the
fall of a sparrow** (cf. Matthew 10:29 "Are not two sparrows sold for a
farthing? and one of them shall not fall on the ground without your Father")   225 **betimes** early

Hamlet. Give me your pardon, sir. I have done you
    wrong,
  But pardon't, as you are a gentleman.
  This presence° knows, and you must needs have
    heard,
230 How I am punished with a sore distraction.
  What I have done
  That might your nature, honor, and exception°
  Roughly awake, I here proclaim was madness.
  Was't Hamlet wronged Laertes? Never Hamlet.
235 If Hamlet from himself be ta'en away,
  And when he's not himself does wrong Laertes,
  Then Hamlet does it not, Hamlet denies it.
  Who does it then? His madness. If't be so,
  Hamlet is of the faction° that is wronged;
240 His madness is poor Hamlet's enemy.
  Sir, in this audience,
  Let my disclaiming from a purposed evil
  Free me so far in your most generous thoughts
  That I have shot my arrow o'er the house
  And hurt my brother.

245 *Laertes.*   I am satisfied in nature,
  Whose motive in this case should stir me most
  To my revenge. But in my terms of honor
  I stand aloof, and will no reconcilement
  Till by some elder masters of known honor
250 I have a voice and precedent° of peace
  To keep my name ungored. But till that time
  I do receive your offered love like love,
  And will not wrong it.

Hamlet.   I embrace it freely,
  And will this brother's wager frankly play.
  Give us the foils. Come on.

255 *Laertes.*   Come, one for me.

Hamlet. I'll be your foil,° Laertes. In mine ignorance

229 **presence** royal assembly   232 **exception** disapproval   239 **faction**
party, side   250 **voice and precedent** authoritative opinion justified by
precedent   256 **foil** (1) blunt sword (2) background (of metallic leaf)
for a jewel

Your skill shall, like a star i' th' darkest night,
Stick fiery off° indeed.

Laertes.   You mock me, sir.

Hamlet. No, by this hand.

King. Give them the foils, young Osric. Cousin Hamlet, 260
You know the wager?

Hamlet.   Very well, my lord.
Your grace has laid the odds o' th' weaker side.

King. I do not fear it, I have seen you both;
But since he is bettered,° we have therefore odds.

Laertes. This is too heavy; let me see another. 265

Hamlet. This likes me well. These foils have all a
length?

                         Prepare to play.

Osric. Ay, my good lord.

King. Set me the stoups of wine upon that table.
If Hamlet give the first or second hit,
Or quit° in answer of the third exchange, 270
Let all the battlements their ordnance fire.
The King shall drink to Hamlet's better breath,
And in the cup an union° shall he throw
Richer than that which four successive kings
In Denmark's crown have worn. Give me the cups, 275
And let the kettle° to the trumpet speak,
The trumpet to the cannoneer without,
The cannons to the heavens, the heaven to earth,
"Now the King drinks to Hamlet." Come, begin.
                         Trumpets the while.
And you, the judges, bear a wary eye. 280

Hamlet. Come on, sir.

Laertes.   Come, my lord.   *They play.*

Hamlet.   One.

Laertes.   No.

258 **Stick fiery off** stand out brilliantly 264 **bettered** has improved (?)
is regarded as better by the public (?) 270 **quit** repay, hit back
273 **union** pearl 276 **kettle** kettledrum

Hamlet.   Judgment?

Osric. A hit, a very palpable hit.
　　Drum, trumpets, and shot. Flourish; a piece goes off.

Laertes.   Well, again.

King. Stay, give me drink. Hamlet, this pearl is thine.
　　Here's to thy health. Give him the cup.

285 *Hamlet.* I'll play this bout first; set it by awhile.
　　Come. [*They play.*] Another hit. What say you?

Laertes. A touch, a touch; I do confess't.

King. Our son shall win.

Queen.   He's fat,° and scant of breath.
　　Here, Hamlet, take my napkin, rub thy brows.
290　　The Queen carouses to thy fortune, Hamlet.

Hamlet. Good madam!

King.   Gertrude, do not drink.

Queen. I will, my lord; I pray you pardon me. [*Drinks.*]

King. [*Aside*] It is the poisoned cup; it is too late.

Hamlet. I dare not drink yet, madam—by and by.

295 *Queen.* Come, let me wipe thy face.

Laertes. My lord, I'll hit him now.

King.   I do not think't.

Laertes. [*Aside*] And yet it is almost against my con-
　　science.

Hamlet. Come for the third, Laertes. You do but dally.
　　I pray you pass with your best violence;
300　　I am sure you make a wanton° of me.

Laertes. Say you so? Come on.   [*They*] *play.*

Osric. Nothing neither way.

Laertes. Have at you now!
　　　In scuffling they change rapiers, [and both are
　　　　　　　　　　　　　　　　　　　wounded].

288 **fat** (1) sweaty (2) out of training   300 **wanton** spoiled child

King.   Part them. They are incensed.

Hamlet. Nay, come—again!   [*The Queen falls.*]

Osric.   Look to the Queen there, ho!

Horatio. They bleed on both sides. How is it, my lord?   305

Osric. How is't, Laertes?

Laertes. Why, as a woodcock to mine own springe,°
    Osric.
    I am justly killed with mine own treachery.

Hamlet. How does the Queen?

King.   She sounds° to see them bleed.

Queen. No, no, the drink, the drink! O my dear
    Hamlet!   310
    The drink, the drink! I am poisoned.   [*Dies.*]

Hamlet. O villainy! Ho! Let the door be locked.
    Treachery! Seek it out.   [*Laertes falls.*]

Laertes. It is here, Hamlet. Hamlet, thou art slain;
    No med'cine in the world can do thee good.   315
    In thee there is not half an hour's life.
    The treacherous instrument is in thy hand,
    Unbated and envenomed. The foul practice°
    Hath turned itself on me. Lo, here I lie,
    Never to rise again. Thy mother's poisoned.   320
    I can no more. The King, the King's to blame.

Hamlet. The point envenomed too?
    Then, venom, to thy work.   *Hurts the King.*

All. Treason! Treason!

King. O, yet defend me, friends. I am but hurt.   325

Hamlet. Here, thou incestuous, murd'rous, damnèd
    Dane,
    Drink off this potion. Is thy union° here?
    Follow my mother.   *King dies.*

Laertes.   He is justly served.

---

307 **springe** snare 309 **sounds** swoons 318 **practice** deception
327 **union** (1) the pearl put into the drink in 5.2.273; (2) the King's
poisonous (incestuous) marriage

It is a poison tempered° by himself.
330 Exchange forgiveness with me, noble Hamlet.
Mine and my father's death come not upon thee,
Nor thine on me!   *Dies.*

Hamlet. Heaven make thee free of it! I follow thee.
I am dead, Horatio. Wretched Queen, adieu!
335 You that look pale and tremble at this chance,
That are but mutes° or audience to this act,
Had I but time (as this fell sergeant,° Death,
Is strict in his arrest) O, I could tell you—
But let it be. Horatio, I am dead;
340 Thou livest; report me and my cause aright
To the unsatisfied.°

Horatio.   Never believe it.
I am more an antique Roman° than a Dane.
Here's yet some liquor left.

Hamlet.   As th' art a man,
Give me the cup. Let go. By heaven, I'll ha't!
345 O God, Horatio, what a wounded name,
Things standing thus unknown, shall live behind me!
If thou didst ever hold me in thy heart,
Absent thee from felicity° awhile,
And in this harsh world draw thy breath in pain,
To tell my story.   *A march afar off.* [*Exit Osric.*]
350   What warlike noise is this?

                                      Enter Osric.

Osric. Young Fortinbras, with conquest come from
    Poland,
To th' ambassadors of England gives
This warlike volley.

Hamlet.   O, I die, Horatio!
The potent poison quite o'ercrows° my spirit.
355 I cannot live to hear the news from England,

---

329 **tempered** mixed   336 **mutes** performers who have no words to
speak   337 **fell sergeant** dread sheriff's officer   341 **unsatisfied** unin-
formed   342 **antique Roman** (with reference to the old Roman fashion
of suicide)   348 **felicity** i.e., the felicity of death   354 **o'ercrows** over-
powers (as a triumphant cock crows over its weak opponent)

But I do prophesy th' election lights
On Fortinbras. He has my dying voice.
So tell him, with th' occurrents,° more and less,
Which have solicited°—the rest is silence.   *Dies.*

Horatio. Now cracks a noble heart. Good night, sweet
    Prince,   *360*
And flights of angels sing thee to thy rest.
                                              [March within.]
Why does the drum come hither?

    Enter Fortinbras, with the Ambassadors with
        Drum, Colors, and Attendants.

Fortinbras. Where is this sight?

Horatio.   What is it you would see?
If aught of woe or wonder, cease your search.

Fortinbras. This quarry° cries on havoc.° O proud
    Death,   *365*
What feast is toward° in thine eternal cell
That thou so many princes at a shot
So bloodily hast struck?

Ambassador.   The sight is dismal;
And our affairs from England come too late.
The ears are senseless that should give us hearing   *370*
To tell him his commandment is fulfilled,
That Rosencrantz and Guildenstern are dead.
Where should we have our thanks?

Horatio.   Not from his° mouth,
Had it th' ability of life to thank you.
He never gave commandment for their death.   *375*
But since, so jump° upon this bloody question,
You from the Polack wars, and you from England,
Are here arrived, give order that these bodies
High on a stage° be placèd to the view,
And let me speak to th' yet unknowing world   *380*
How these things came about. So shall you hear

358 **occurrents** occurrences   359 **solicited** incited   365 **quarry** heap
of slain bodies   365 **cries on havoc** proclaims general slaughter
366 **toward** in preparation   373 **his** (Claudius')   376 **jump** precisely
379 **stage** platform

Of carnal, bloody, and unnatural acts,
Of accidental judgments, casual° slaughters,
Of deaths put on by cunning and forced cause,
385   And, in this upshot, purposes mistook
Fall'n on th' inventors' heads. All this can I
Truly deliver.

Fortinbras.   Let us haste to hear it,
And call the noblest to the audience.
For me, with sorrow I embrace my fortune.
390   I have some rights of memory° in this kingdom,
Which now to claim my vantage doth invite me.

Horatio. Of that I shall have also cause to speak,
And from his mouth whose voice will draw on°
   more.
But let this same be presently performed,
Even while men's minds are wild, lest more mis-
395   chance
On° plots and errors happen.

Fortinbras.   Let four captains
Bear Hamlet like a soldier to the stage,
For he was likely, had he been put on,°
To have proved most royal; and for his passage°
400   The soldiers' music and the rite of war
Speak loudly for him.
Take up the bodies. Such a sight as this
Becomes the field,° but here shows much amiss.
Go, bid the soldiers shoot.

Exeunt marching; after the which a peal of ordnance
are shot off.

FINIS

---

383 **casual** not humanly planned, chance   390 **rights of memory** remembered claims   393 **voice will draw on** vote will influence
396 **On** on top of   398 **put on** advanced (to the throne)   399 **passage**
death   403 **field** battlefield